I0713634

FLORENCE WITKOP

STAR PORTAL

by

Florence Witkop

ISBN-13: 978-1-959788-87-4

CHAPTER 1

Wyoming.

Finally.

Not just Wyoming, but the property my family now owned that I was checking out. A ranch. A real-life, western ranch in a remote location with an actual log cabin and no near neighbors. A ranch inherited from my hermit uncle who, according to family lore, had a secret.

I'd heard about the secret forever. It was a family legend. As soon as I heard about the ranch, I vowed to uncover that secret if I ever had a chance to see the ranch itself.

Now that I was actually there, however, instead of rushing to find out whether there truly was a secret or not and, if so, what it was, I just stared at the ranch. It had taken longer than necessary to get there because, as I drove, I considered another side to the whole inherited-a-place-with-a-secret thing. Maybe the secret sucked. So I'd dawdled. Taken side trips. And so on.

Staring through the windshield, the ranch looked lonely and scary empty. The kind of place where anything could happen. And would. A place where secrets lurked in every corner and crevice. Scary secrets. And I was alone.

When I'd finally turned off the freeway onto the dirt roads that were all there was beyond civilization and with my imagination working overtime, I was barely crawling. When I reached the end of my trip along what was closer to a cow path than a road, instead of going immediately to what would be my home for the foreseeable future, I put the car in neutral and coasted. And then stopped.

I told myself I was tired and my body was screaming for a rest and that justified pulling to the side of the seldom-used rutted road and turning off the engine instead of finishing the last quarter mile of my journey. As the engine died, I just sat with my hands on the steering wheel to stop their trembling and stared at the cabin that would be my home for the foreseeable future and remembered how it had happened. How I'd actually ended up in such an unlikely place.

~

"You should go," my mother had said in a voice so sweet I knew she'd had an ulterior motive as she'd smoothed butter-cream frosting over a sheet cake and set it aside for whomever was going to pick it up for whatever special occasion they were about to celebrate with the help of our family bakery.

"You're the oldest and done with school," she'd said. "You're intelligent and educated. You shouldn't stay with us forever. We can manage without you. You should move out. You should go somewhere and the ranch is as good place as any to start your adult life. You can spend the whole summer there if you choose. Or forever if you find it's right for you, never to return."

I'd stuck a finger in the left-over frosting and licked it as I listed my many reasons for not going. I'd always been a responsible daughter and the busy season lay ahead. "It's almost summer. Tourists by the dozen. Birthdays, the Fourth of July, and so on. I'm the only one of us kids with no scheduled summer activities and you can't afford to pay someone. So you need me."

I'd swiped another finger through the frosting and ignored my mother's frown as I continued. "The younger kids are already scheduled for the entire summer what with baseball, swimming, art and so forth because you believe in a well-rounded education, and I've already done those things but my younger siblings haven't. You can't ask them to give up their summer so I can check out our late uncle's ranch."

I'd watched to see how she'd react because that reaction could very well decide what I'd be doing that summer. Her expression had said my concerns had already been discussed and dealt with. "We'll manage and someone should go and it must be now, in the summer, because the roads out there are dangerous in the winter and mostly impassible."

"No cell service and no phone. We'll be unable to communicate. What if something goes wrong?"

"You have gobs of common sense."

"No electricity except for a generator."

"Which you know how to operate."

"Wyoming is far from Illinois and the ranch is isolated."

The gleam in my mother's eyes said she knew exactly how conflicted I was and that she'd beat down any objections I might have because she and my dad believed in grabbing the brass ring and the ranch in Wyoming was shining brightly with my name writ in large letters. "There's a neighbor. Bridger is the last name, I believe. He's caring for Cantrell's dog."

"Which I'll have to pick up so I'll have to meet him and you're sneakily suggesting that when I get the dog I casually mention in passing that of course we'll depend on one another. Neighbors and all."

She'd grinned. "Something like that." With which she'd stuck the frosting bowl in the dishwasher, threw the towels in the laundry and switched off the lights with a finality that meant I was going to Wyoming.

Not too many days later I pulled out of our driveway in the tiny car that had served me well in

Illinois and would probably have a panic attack the moment I reached the mountains of Wyoming. It was loaded to the roof with just about everything I owned because none of us had any idea what I'd find when I reached Uncle Cantrell's ranch.

I took a deep breath as I pulled onto the freeway and tried to prepare myself for whatever the summer would bring. Secrets and all.

I drove carefully, almost sedately, and told myself I was doing so because I was being responsible instead of because my eagerness was mixed with fear of the coming summer alone in a remote area and I didn't know which was stronger. Fear or excitement.

I called home at the last tiny town before reaching the ranch to let everyone know I'd talked with Uncle Cantrell's lawyer and gotten the keys to the cabin. Not that I needed them, he'd said. No one locked their doors. Probably wouldn't even work.

It was my last call before losing cell service so my dad ran me through how to operate the generator that would provide minimal electricity. For the hundredth time. Until he was sure I knew what to do. How to have power. I told him the lawyer said there was plenty of fuel so I didn't need to get any in town. Just groceries.

Then we hung up and I shoved the now useless cell phone into my suitcase, checked the hand-drawn map the lawyer had given me, and headed into a region of forested mountains interspersed with open spaces where the wind swept hard and dry across miles of brown terrain.

It didn't feel as though I was climbing but my poor car protested enough that I knew I must be. I slowed down to give the overworked thing a break and enjoy the scenery as a totally unexpected feeling of surprise and freedom took over. It started somewhere in my middle and grew with each curve in the road that opened onto a broad vista of the west. I hadn't expected to actually like this part of the country. But I did.

Perhaps I was reading too much into the 'secrets' thing. Because, looking through the windshield, I realized that this wide-open country could be what I'd always wanted. What the entire family knew I wanted even though I'd never said a word. Perhaps Uncle Cantrell's secret was that he lived in a rough-shod version of paradise.

I found the ranch easily enough and that was when I stopped far enough away to take a deep breath, reorient myself, and get a good look at the place where I'd be living. It consisted of a small cabin tucked against a hill with a tiny stream crossing what would have been a yard if there'd been anything resembling grass or flowers or any other thing that spoke of civilization. Instead there was just wilderness and cabin juxtaposed together in perfect harmony with a slightly larger building to one side of the cabin that could have been a barn or tool shed or something else entirely.

Everything appeared neat and well cared for but it was growing late and I had a lot of stuff to lug into the cabin so I stopped staring, decided I was more adventurous than afraid of a secret that might not exist, and started the car once more.

I decided to check the outbuilding in the morning because I was not only unexpectedly upbeat I was suddenly hungry and needed to figure out how to make a meal. What kind of stove Uncle Cantrell had used and whether I'd know how to work it. I'd brought lots of sandwich stuff and expected maybe that would be what I'd have for dinner.

I parked close to the cabin porch to make unloading easier. Inside I discovered the stove burned wood. I knew how to make a fire because back home we used our fireplace often and roasted marshmallows in the backyard fire pit.

Uncle Cantrell had left the necessary things to get a fire going piled neatly near the stove but far enough away not to be dangerous. Soon I had a fire going that was hot enough for cooking. The heat was welcome because, though it was warm outside, the inside of the cabin was cool enough to make me think the nights might be cold. Summer might come late in the mountains. I didn't know enough about Wyoming to know one way or the other.

I had hot soup for dinner and found the single bedroom clean and comfortable with an assortment of truly warm comforters to choose from that made me wonder just how cold it got in the winter. And maybe all year around. Seeing all those blankets, I hesitated before finally deciding to let the fire go out and the cabin grow cold. Surely the comforters would keep me warm.

Still, in an abundance of caution, I piled extra comforters next to the bed to grab if I became chilled during the night. I also put my next day's clothes close enough to grab them and dress beneath the covers if it was really cold. Heavy jeans, boots, a long-sleeved shirt, and a cowboy hat I'd bought in the last town because everyone seemed to be wearing one. Almost as an afterthought, I added a sheepskin vest to the pile. Just in case.

It turned out that the cabin held heat well. Though it was cold outside the next morning, it was warm enough in the cabin that I didn't need the extra comforters or the sheepskin vest. Another fire in the stove to prepare breakfast warmed the entire building enough that I judged it would remain comfortable all day.

The day's outfit had been chosen for whatever I was likely to find in the Wyoming back country. Snakes. Thorny bushes. Sun that felt warm and nice and would burn me to a crisp without sunblock even though the air was crisp and cool. I'd read about Wyoming.

The cowboy hat had been a good addition to my wardrobe. In short, I was prepared and that made me feel good and suddenly, as I looked through the window to the bright day beyond, in a complete about face from how I'd felt during the trip, I felt both competent and adventurous. My parents had been right to push me out of the nest.

The building behind the cabin turned out to be for everything except living. Storage. As a repair shop. It held two large freezers powered by the huge generator I knew how to use thanks to those mini classes from my dad. Diesel fuel was in drums a safe space away from both buildings. No chance of starting either place on fire. My respect for my deceased uncle increased with every new thing I found.

With the place figured out, I turned back to the hand-drawn map with directions to the neighbor's place to pick up Uncle Cantrell's dog. Another place without a phone, most likely, so I couldn't tell him in advance that I was coming. I'd have to just show up and hope he was home.

CHAPTER 2

I climbed into my tiny car and headed over a low ridge followed by two hills covered with scrubby brush and then still more hills and more brush to my next-door neighbor's place. A lot of miles, I decided, and wondered if long distances were common between ranches in this remote part of Wyoming. Probably. But the scenery was lovely, wild and stark, and I drove slowly enough to take it all in.

I'd been there less than a full day and, in a full about-face from my previous hesitation, had decided I wanted Wyoming to become a part of me. To sink into my soul. I was an introvert and this place was made for solitude. Hermits welcome, adventure would be an added perk that seemed to be waiting around every curve in the road.

The ranch where I was to pick up Uncle Cantrell's dog was almost a duplicate of the ranch I'd just left, only slightly larger. A cabin with one outbuilding but this outbuilding was considerably larger than my uncle's. Maybe large enough to be a barn and there was a lean-to on the back of it that was as large as my uncle's entire second building that could serve the same function as that second building on Uncle Cantrell's ranch. Or more. But the cabin itself was about the same size.

I drove close to the cabin and parked in what I hoped was an acceptable spot but I couldn't know because, like at Uncle Cantrell's ranch, there was no defined yard and no discernable parking area. Just bare ground with wild grasses that were green and yellow and brown with rocks strewn about here and there. The result was lovely in a way I'd not thought could possibly be lovely. But it was.

I got out and wondered where to start looking for the owner. I needn't have bothered because my car engine had hardly died when a man stepped out of the cabin. Tallish, muscular from outdoor living with brown hair that needed a haircut and a totally male no-nonsense, put-together way about him. He was wearing clothes that were a duplicate of what I wore. Jeans, boots, and a long-sleeved shirt. I was sure there was a cowboy hat somewhere in the cabin that he'd grab before he went anywhere.

"Hi," he said in a pleasant baritone. No hint of an accent so no way to know where he was from. "You here for the dog?"

"How'd you know?"

"Easy enough." He laughed, a comfortable sound

in the crystal air that invited me to relax. How'd he see that I was nervous? And why was I? There was no reason for it. I was a normal person on a normal errand. But I felt somehow weird in the wide-open land and now I knew my nerves were obvious to anyone who looked. Unless his acuity was a trait specific to him. Or a Wyoming thing. Perhaps the solitude made inhabitants better able to read their occasional guests.

My face flushed as I realized he was standing there reading me like a book, emotions and all. Then he explained how he knew who I was. "You're driving a tiny car that can only be from a city and the family that inherited Cantrell's ranch is from a city. Somewhere in Illinois, I believe. So it wasn't hard to figure out who you are. Besides, I don't get a lot of company so there weren't many possibilities. No one does out here."

His head tilted a bit as he added, "This country doesn't lend itself to people wandering all over the place. But I knew someone would come eventually to get Midnight."

"Midnight? Is that the dog's name?" I considered his expression. Eyes lit with intelligence. A mobile mouth. A slight, comfortable smile. My new neighbor might be a nice man. A decent person. Then I felt stupid because of course he was a decent person. He was caring for my uncle's dog and he didn't have to do that. "You're right. I'm here for Uncle Cantrell's dog."

"Midnight is around someplace. He likes to go exploring. He might have gone somewhere. He could be gone a while."

"I can come back later."

"No need. If I'd known you were coming to get him today, I'd have kept him in the barn but, unfortunately, without a phone there was no way to know when it would happen." The smile grew. White teeth gleamed briefly. "Come on in. I can make a pot of coffee if you drink coffee and I think I have some cookies if they haven't gone stale."

"I love coffee." I didn't care if the cookies were stale. I was in Wyoming. I'd made it here and I was talking with a real, live cowboy and could spend the whole summer here if I chose. Or forever. As I followed him into the cabin, I found myself thinking I just might do that. In fact, I might do more. I might become a cowgirl myself if such was possible.

"I'm Noah," he said over strong, hot, black coffee and cookies that were sort of edible.

"Emma."

We studied each other. Now that we were out of the bright sun and close enough to see details I saw sun-browned skin and hands rough from physical work but the thing I noticed most was an alertness, as if he saw everything about his surroundings in an instant and tucked that information away somewhere to be pulled out as needed.

There was nothing special about me for him to see. Straw colored hair and everything else as medium as possible. I was the epitome of normal and fidgeted under his inspection. He, on the other hand, improved with each new thing I noticed. His height, the way his head tilted, and his eyes sparked and the fact that he didn't gesture much when he spoke. But though he seemed totally relaxed, it was the stillness of a coiled spring.

My mother had been right. This man could be a handy person to know. He definitely gave out competent vibes and I was glad he'd be nearby if serious problems arose though I'd never ask for help for anything less than an actual catastrophe. Not my style. I'm determinedly self-sufficient.

But it was hard to pull my eyes away until I realized I was staring way longer than was polite. Then I flushed and forced myself to look over the inside of the cabin. As neat as Uncle Cantrell's place, with what must be a bedroom as the only other room and open shelves everywhere filled with the necessities of life in the country.

The whole time I checked him over and after I'd looked away, his eyes examined me. I could feel them on me and decided to take the focus off me by putting it on him. "What do you do so far from everywhere? Do you own cattle?" A normal assumption in the rural west.

He didn't act like I was being nosy, merely shaking his head. "Not cattle. Horses. I'm okay with horses and a fair rider so I train horses and teach riders how to ride better."

"Like a rodeo thing?"

"Just normal riding. For cattle roundups and pleasure." His eyes sparked. "I like horses and I like people as long as there aren't too many at any one time."

A good person to know indeed. If my goal of becoming a cowgirl was to be filled, he was the place to start.

I lapsed into silence but he continued to look at me. He had something on his mind and it wasn't horses. I learned what it was when he said, "It's none of my business but I have a question if you don't mind."

"What do you want to know?"

"Your uncle was a nice guy. A good neighbor. I liked him a lot. But he seemed to have a secret."

"Uncle Cantrell? A secret?" So it wasn't just a family legend. But did I want to tell a stranger what I'd been told? Maybe not. "I have no idea about that. So I can't guess what it might have been or even if one really existed."

He got up and moved about the largish room, pouring himself another cup of coffee before sitting down once more and replacing his feet on a chair in an impression of ease that wouldn't fool anyone. "It's probably nothing. A personality quirk. A vibe he gave off that there was more to him than what could be seen." It was clear that he truly believed my late uncle had been hiding something.

But I still wasn't comfortable saying anything.

"Sorry but I know nothing about any secret and no one in our family knows anything either. Like you said, probably just a vibe." On the other hand, Uncle Cantrell might have confided in this man enough to provide a hint about the secret. "Did he ever say anything?"

He shook his head. "Nope. Nothing. I was most likely just imagining it." But his expression said it was more than a vibe Uncle Cantrell gave off. He'd been hiding something.

A sound interrupted us. A scratching at the door. "Here's Midnight." He opened the door and in walked the largest black Labrador retriever I'd ever seen in my life who looked me over and started towards me but stopped a few feet away. "Here," Noah said, tossing me a broken piece of cookie. "Give it to him. He's a foodie and he'll love you forever."

Soon Midnight and I were friends. "Thanks,"

"No thanks needed. Midnight is a good doggie. And a sweetheart."

"He's huge."

"The biggest Lab I've ever seen."

"Everything out here seems to be big."

That smile again and a chuckle. "I guess Wyoming is different than where you're from."

"Totally."

He studied me some more only this time the inspection was open and completely friendly. When it was done, I hoped we were friends. A friend would be nice, possibly essential. He asked, "Do you ride?"

"Huh?"

"Horses? Do you ride horses?"

"Yes, but I doubt my skill level would be considered acceptable around here." Our neighbors had horses and loved kids so all the kids in the neighborhood learned the fundamentals. But I'd never gotten further than that. I wasn't a cowgirl. Yet.

"It's early. Lots of daytime left. We can go for a ride if you like. You can get to know the countryside. I can show you around your property." He stopped, then continued, "If you want. If you have the time."

"I'd like that." And of course, I had time. Time stretched open and inviting in this land that felt disconnected from the rest of the world. Midnight begged for another cookie, and I gave him a second piece. "But what about Midnight?"

"He can come too. He'll love it." He examined the huge Lab. "He'll be good to have along. Large, competent, and protective of his people." He looked at me over his coffee. "Which will be you once he gets to know you better. A ride will be a good time for the two of you to start the process." With which he grabbed the wide-brimmed cowboy hat I knew had to be somewhere in the cabin, plopped it on his head, strapped a pistol around his waist, and led the way outside.

Turned out the second building was a barn, as I'd thought. Empty stalls because the horses were outside, several western saddles and a lot of tack along one side. A couple of cats watched from the loft. "I'll get the horses."

"Are they far away?"

"In the corral." I flushed. I'd not noticed the barbed wire fence behind the barn and the horses were in a thicket of evergreen trees so I'd not seen them either. "They like the shade." He opened the corral gate and walked through. I followed. "You can wait here if you want."

"I'd like to go with you." The cowgirl thing. If I was to learn how to do cowgirl things this was a good time to start my education as well as a good time to get close to Midnight. "Get to know the horse I'll be riding," I added, as if an explanation was needed, but it was the truth.

I wasn't a good enough rider to climb on board just any horse and have it go where it was told. I was glad Noah would be around if it decided to go somewhere else. Mostly I hoped his look of competency wasn't an act and that his horses were well trained.

They were. I suspected he picked the most laid-back one for me, a pinto named Cutie Pie with a straight back and a rocking gate that put me at ease. As we headed into the scrub brush that seemed to be the entirety of the nearby landscape, I patted her neck. She replied with a comfortable grunt and didn't speed up even a little bit which was fine with me.

The day was warm, the sun bright, the breeze perfect and I enjoyed every moment of the trip. We rode the boundary of my new property. Then we rode the boundary of Noah's ranch. "Is it all scrub brush?"

"Not all. There are some interesting rock formations not far from here. They are mostly on your property though some are on mine. Your uncle said the area reminded him of days gone by. Before the area was settled." He turned his horse towards a formation a short ride away.

Cutie Pie followed without me having to do anything. She was a nice, sweet horse. A docile follower. Thankfully. "It'll be level ground one minute and rocks thirty feet high the next and they'll look like they were piled one on top of another. As if they were dropped from the sky and that was how they landed."

We reached the rocks, and they did, indeed, stand in stark contrast to the surrounding area. The horses stopped as if they made this trip often and knew when we'd arrived. They started grazing on the sparse grass. I started to dismount but Noah put out a hand, reaching across the space between us, and stopped me. "Let me make sure it's safe."

I looked around. "Safe from what?"

"Whatever. Cougars, possibly. More likely rattlesnakes." He rode next to a boulder taller than his horse and scooped up a handful of small rocks that he threw around. "Chasing away any snakes." I was glad he was there and finally realized why he had a pistol strapped to his waist. I had a lot to learn about life out west.

I didn't dismount until after Noah was off his horse

and had walked around a bit. Then I climbed down gingerly and looked around and only moved away from trusty Cutie Pie after I'd thoroughly inspected the nearby ground. It seemed okay and the fact that Midnight was nosing around all over the place gave me confidence that there were no nasty surprises ready to jump out at me.

I joined Noah and ignored his almost-smile at my tenderfoot ways. "You were right. The rocks are interesting." I went up to the closest one. Scrub brush covered most of it and prevented me from getting right next to it. But I could look.

I pointed. "That formation in the rock. It's shaped like a door."

He followed my finger. "You're right. It's a perfect door shape. In the rock."

The longer we stared the more we recognized the indentation in the rock face of the formation as a concise replica of a door. Not a door itself, of course. That was impossible. Wasn't it?

CHAPTER 3

The precisely rectangular indentation was barely visible behind brush that cascaded over the rock formation. But when we knew what to look for, it was obvious.

"It looks like we could step right through."

Noah squinted. "It's exactly like a door. Sharp corners, correct dimensions, and all. It even has a doorknob or something similar where a doorknob would be." A large door of a size people would use to enter a stadium. It was a perfect replica of a door. We gazed at it for a long moment. "If that brush was gone, we'd be able to get close and see it better."

"Thorns. Lots of them."

Just then a jack rabbit zipped past. It ran straight into the brush alongside the strange formation. Midnight followed, barking loudly. The huge Lab didn't let the brush stop him. He ran straight into it after the jack rabbit, and we watched to see which animal would win this contest.

The rabbit scrambled up a narrow ledge and disappeared over the top of the rock formation, safe from Midnight. The dog howled in frustration but didn't leave. Instead, he nosed around, looking for a way to go after the jack rabbit.

As he moved, the brush moved with him. He was a large dog, and the entire bush came away from the rock formation and fell over, leaving Midnight standing next to the door-like shape. We stared at the newly bare rock. Noah spoke first. "The brush just fell over. There are no roots to hold it in place."

"It's artificial." We were both stunned. In the middle of the vastness of Wyoming's back country someone had placed artificial greenery against a rock formation that was as out of place as the artificial greenery in front of it. "It was just propped against the rock."

"To hide it?"

"I can't think of any other reason."

"Why?" We both asked the question at the same time and moved in unison to examine the oddity.

If we didn't look too closely, what had looked like a doorknob now seemed more like the electronic locks some cars have. Midnight watched us examine the formation. Looked from us and then to what resembled a door. Knew the indentation in the rock was important to us because of the way we were staring at it and if it was important to his people then it was important to him.

So, the Lab went to the door and sniffed. Then walked from one side to the other, puzzled about this thing a couple of humans were paying so much attention to. Then he scratched at it as if doing so would tell him what was so important about a largish slab of rock. Then he scratched harder though the rock was so hard he left no marks.

"Hey, boy," Noah said and reached for Midnight to pull him away. "You'll wear yourself out trying to dig a hole in solid rock."

He didn't pull Midnight away from the rock. He couldn't because the second his hand touched Midnight's collar something happened. The dog, having been pushing against the rock, simply went through it as if it didn't exist. As if it was a hologram instead of solid rock. And Noah's hand and arm went through too.

Noah pulled back quickly but didn't have a good enough grip on Midnight's collar to haul him back with him so Midnight went all the way through what was now something insubstantial. And disappeared.

But we could hear him barking from the other side.

"Come, boy. Come Midnight." Noah's voice showed alarm. Perhaps panic. Calm, collected Noah couldn't wrap his mind around what had just happened.

I was too stunned to do anything. I couldn't even move. But Noah quickly, with that mental agility I'd noticed to instantly be aware of what was happening around him and act accordingly, got his act together and leaned forward. He called the dog back.

We heard scratching. Midnight was on the other side of whatever that thing was, and he wanted to return. But he couldn't. It had turned solid again and he was stuck there. He whined. He wanted us to help.

Noah and I stared at each other. Noah's face hardened. "I'm going to get him. I can't leave him there. Wherever he is. I won't." He reached towards the door and, just as before, his arm went right through to the other side. He bit his lip and said, "If he can't come here then I'm going there."

"Don't." I found my voice. "We don't know what it is. It could be deadly. What if you can't come back?"

His eyes narrowed. "I'll come back, and I'll bring Midnight back with me." He took a deep breath, turned to me and in a different voice, one I'd not heard before, said, "But if I don't, if the worst happens, Cutie Pie knows the way home." And he stepped through. And disappeared.

Just like that. One minute we were on horses exploring the ranch my family had inherited and the next my companion had walked through solid rock.

I held my breath. Looked at the blue sky and a lone bird flying above and the horses grazing calmly nearby. And couldn't believe what had just happened. Noah should be standing beside me and Midnight beside him. But they weren't. They were gone.

Moments later, they both stepped back through that door-like slab of rock, Noah holding Midnight's collar.

I breathed again. "You're back."

"It was easy." He turned to examine the rock face again. "It was easy for me. I just stepped through and it was as if the rock wasn't there. As if it was an open door. But Midnight couldn't get through. It was solid rock for him." His shoulders lifted and dropped. "Until I thought to help him through and then everything was okay. We could walk through together."

I looked from dog to man, both just returned from someplace that didn't exist and then to the indentation in the rock that was now just another rock formation, albeit an unusual one. "Let's get out of here." All the bravado of a new place was gone. I was off balance and queasy.

"Good idea." Noah led the way to the horses and soon we were on our way back to his ranch. Neither of us said a word during the entire ride. Nor did we speak while we dismounted and walked the horses to cool them down and then brushed them clean and put the saddles and other tack away.

But when we were inside and he was making the second pot of coffee that day, as he bent over the stove and pretended to be fascinated by the coffee pot, he said slowly, in a way that said he'd been thinking about it the whole time, "What happened out there was interesting. And I suspect we unintentionally uncovered your uncle's secret."

He went still, waiting for me to comment and eventually I did. "What exactly was the most interesting thing about it?" Terrifying, perhaps. Impossible. But interesting?

We looked each other over like fighters warily circling one another only we were sparring verbally instead of physically as we tried to come to grips with what had just happened. We both wanted to talk about it. We needed to talk about it. But at the same time, neither of us knew how to discuss it rationally. We literally didn't know what to say about something that couldn't happen but did.

When the coffee was finally ready and we were across from each other at the table with a cup for each of us, he said, "The other side. That's what was interesting." He was prompting me. He wanted me to say something. Anything.

I looked at him over the rim of my cup, through the steam rising from it. Hot, black, strong coffee. A jolt of reality. Just what I needed. "You weren't there very long."

"Long enough."

I didn't want to continue the conversation. I wanted to forget the whole thing. Instead, because I couldn't help myself, I asked, "What was it like? The other side?"

"Different." His face was distorted by the steam except there wasn't much steam so maybe it was the dimness of the cabin that turned him into something unreal. More likely it was that something had just happened that was impossible and had thrown my entire world out of focus, including the man across the table. Then man who not much earlier had seemed the epitome of reality.

I didn't keep quiet. I had to ask. Had a thousand questions because I couldn't undo what had happened and couldn't unsee what had been seen and couldn't forget an experience like the one we'd just had. "Different in what way?" I braced for his answer.

"Wherever that place is, it isn't Wyoming. Massive shade trees and grass that was actually green. Pleasantly warm. And I thought I saw a lake in the distance. Or an ocean. With a beach."

"A normal enough scene."

"Normal but in a way it wasn't normal, not for anyplace I can think of, though I couldn't say precisely what was wrong. But there was a wrongness. Or maybe just a difference."

"We mustn't go back. We should pile rocks around the doorway so no one can ever find it. We must never return. Ever."

He looked at me over the rim of his cup and gulped a big shot of coffee before answering. Because, like me, he needed that jolt of caffeine to deal with what had happened. "But we will return and you know that as well as I do." He took another shot of coffee and waited for it to pool in his stomach and warm his insides. "You know that we will go back. I see it in your face. We will return because we won't be able to ignore the doorway in the middle of nowhere that goes somewhere else. Not now that we've seen it and know it's there. We can't."

His eyes narrowed as he thought about what he'd just said. "And it is a doorway. A portal of some kind. We both know that as surely as we both know we're going to return and find out what's on the other side."

He was right. I'd just refused to acknowledge it. But I was still afraid. "We're going to walk through together. I hope."

He nodded and just like that, a pact was made. An agreement that was long and complicated and made without a word being said but we both knew what the pact involved. A return to the portal. An admission that doing so could be dangerous, even deadly, but we'd do it anyway because we couldn't live with ourselves if we didn't. An acknowledgement of our burning desire to know what was beyond that portal. And an agreement not to tell anyone anything about it because they'd laugh us out of existence.

Noah spoke, skipping past our silent agreement in his need to figure out how to accomplish the impossible task we'd set ourselves. "First we figure out why I could go through the portal but Midnight couldn't."

"Agreed."

"At first only one of us goes through at a time. Just in case. And we take a rope that'll be anchored in this place."

"This world. This reality." It was the first time I said the words and they tasted odd and sounded exotic in the still, Wyoming air. But Noah just nodded. "We hope the rope stays in place and can lead us from one place to another."

Another nod and then he said, "I go through first."

"No way! I'm part of whatever this is and you've already been there."

"Which is why I go first. Because I've been there and know what to expect." He relaxed somewhat even as that heightened awareness of his surrounding that seemed to be a part of him didn't dissipate in the least as I slumped and accepted what he said.

He added, "But I won't stay long. Just long enough to know what's happening with Midnight, why he couldn't go through when I could, and to see in a bit more detail what it's like there. Whether it's a lake or ocean. Possibly more things, some of which might be important."

I refilled my coffee and swirled it to inhale the scent. "Okay. You first. Me soon after." That heightened awareness that was a part of him would be invaluable. He should go first. But I should be an immediate second.

His next question set my body thrumming. "So now that's settled, when do we go?"

"Today?"

He shook his head. "Not enough time left today. Besides there are supplies to gather. Plans to make. The horses need to rest." He put his empty cup on the table to signal that the discussion was about to end. "We'll go tomorrow morning as soon as you can get here. I'll have everything ready."

"Daybreak?"

"Dawn? Yes. That's a good time to visit another world." Without the coffee to hide behind, I saw it in his face. The change. He'd got past his shock now that we had a plan. I saw his eagerness. Anticipation. Most of all I saw that alertness that was so much a part of him multiplied a thousand fold as he contemplated what we were about to do. He could hardly wait.

I, too, wanted to see what was on the other side of the door. I might not be as perfect for the trip as he was but I had just as much right to go through the door. And I might not be as mentally and physically alert but I wasn't a slouch either. I would go through the portal and I'd do it because it was there. And because it had to be a portal to another world.

And it was a portal. Not a simple rock that resembled a door. I let the word roll around in my mind as the possibilities swam through my imagination. "You'd better not stay too long in that other world because if you do, I'll drop the rope and let it stay wherever it falls and I'll be through the door myself. Because I want to see what's on the other side. I deserve to see."

"It's not a door. It's a portal," he said quietly in reply, repeating my thoughts of a moment earlier. Our thinking was synchronized. We were focusing on the same topic. "I know it looks like a door. Some might consider it a door. But we both know it's a portal to someplace else. Some other world. And tomorrow we're going to find out what that world is like."

CHAPTER 4

The next morning the sun rose blood red. As I grabbed everything I could think of that we might need and wondered if I should eat before I left or whether Noah would have breakfast ready, I hoped that sun wasn't a bad omen. I'd not seen a similar dawn since arriving in Wyoming. Of course, it was only my third day, my second morning at my new home so that fact might not mean much. Still, I wished that sun was brighter. More friendly.

Then I wiped that depressing thought from my mind and with Midnight beside me I peeled out of the yard so fast I left rubber on what passed for a lawn. I was that determined to explore the world beyond the portal. I was also scared. Terrified. I could barely control either my car or myself and breathed a prayer of thanks that there was no other car around for me to plow into.

Noah had breakfast waiting. "You're right on

time," he said as he peered through a window at that red sun. But he said nothing, just grabbed a couple plates and gestured for me to join him. So maybe it wasn't a bad omen. Maybe it was just a normal Wyoming morning. I could hope.

We ate quickly. No small talk. No plans because they were already made. Nothing beyond fueling our bodies for whatever the day would bring.

Then we saddled the horses and took off, followed by a pack horse with more equipment than I'd have thought to bring. My pile looked insignificant beside Noah's. He saw me inspecting that pack. "Long way back if we need something we don't have with us."

Midnight ran alongside the horses, leaving to investigate something of interest at least once a mile before returning and running ahead and then circling back to tell us to hurry up. He had that much energy. Having the over-sized Lab along pushed some of my trepidations aside. Noah had said the Lab was protective. That was a good thought.

The rock formation was a splash of white against the barren landscape. Looking at it and knowing what it contained, I no longer thought it resembled a natural formation. Of course I have a huge imagination. Everyone who knew me always said so.

I wondered what Noah thought about the formation but didn't ask because we were riding single file. Then we were there. At the pure white rock formation. We'd arrived. We were ready to find out what the world beyond the portal was like beyond the few seconds worth that Noah had seen before.

We set to work, still without talking because we both knew the plan. Pound a stake into the ground. Tie one end of a rope to the stake and the other to Noah. A long rope, probably a hundred feet in length to allow for more than a cursory glance of the world beyond the portal. Bring Midnight along because of that protective gene but have a leash handy in case it was necessary to prevent him from straying. Make sure a camera was available. Prepare a back-pack for me filled with rations in case things went south and he needed to be rescued. Then walk through the portal, find a good place to survey whatever was in sight, and take a million pictures.

The pictures were important, proof that other world actually existed. Even though we had no intention of showing them to anyone else, we'd have them for ourselves.

"Come back soon," was all I said as he and Midnight headed for the portal. Noah's foot went through easily. But Midnight hit solid rock.

"He went through yesterday." Noah's frown said Midnight should have gone through as easily as he did.

I closed my eyes and recalled the previous day. "Yesterday you were pulling Midnight away from the rock because he'd been scratching it too long. He'd wear himself out scratching solid rock. It was only when you touched him that the rock became a portal and he went through.”

Noah snapped the leash on Midnight and just like that, the dog went through. But Noah momentarily remained in our world. The real world. He looked at the leash that was half in our world and half beyond the portal. “The leash is staying in one piece though it’s in two worlds. So the rope will probably do the same.” And he stepped through. All that remained was a rope that went from the stake to a spot on a rock. It looked ridiculous. And scary.

Noah and Midnight were gone about five minutes, the time we’d determined should be enough to take a lot of pictures. Then, just as planned, he and Midnight stepped back through the portal. Noah had Midnight firmly on a leash so the dog could travel from one world to another.

“It must be programmed for human beings and whatever they have with them so Midnight can only go through if a human is touching him or something on him.”

“Which means the portal was programmed. It was created for human beings.”

“Exactly.” The thought was mind-blowing. We stared at each other until Noah unhooked the rope from his waist and handed me his phone. “I took pictures.”

I looked. He’d taken lots of pictures. Dozens. And they all showed what many people would consider a paradise. Lush vegetation with trees heavy with leaves and flowers everywhere and, yes, there was what looked like an ocean not too far away with a white sand beach.

"I couldn't reach the ocean. The rope wasn't long enough. I was tempted to unhook myself but we can check it out later if we decide it's safe to do so." He added, "And it does seem safe. I felt foolish walking around with a rope around my waist." Then his brow furrowed and he said, "But I kept the darned thing around my waist and you should do the same." His eyes narrowed. He meant it but he tried to make a joke out of it. "In case I have to haul you back."

I looked again at the pictures. "So it's Earth as we wish it would be."

He shook his head. "Not Earth. Definitely not Earth."

There was something about the way he spoke. Something. "What makes you say that?"

"There were three moons in the sky. We only have one. And the sun wasn't like our sun. It was huge, many times larger than our sun. And it was red. Blood red."

"Like our sun this morning. I noticed." I shuddered at the memory.

He shook his head. "It wasn't the same. Our sun turns blazing bright once it rises high enough. You can't look at our sun without damaging your eyes. This sun was different. It was at its zenith. It was in the middle of the sky so it must be noon wherever that world is and the sun was still red as fire. A huge, red, orb. But it wasn't bright."

"So it's not Earth." My stomach lurched.

"Definitely not Earth." His eyes closed momentarily as he thought back to his experience. "And the air felt different. I don't know precisely how it was different but it was. Fresh and crisp but it was more than just not being polluted. It was different. And I felt different while I was there. As if I could run faster and jump higher though I didn't try because that should be for another time. For when we know more and decide to experiment." He added grimly, "We don't know much at this point."

"We know it's not Earth."

"When you go through, don't push the exploration bit. One careful, cautious step at a time."

"Speaking of which, it's my turn."

He nodded. "I believe it's safe."

"It won't matter if it's not. It's still my turn. Even if there are monsters."

He laughed without humor. "I wouldn't be surprised if there are. There could be anything so watch yourself. Think before you do anything. Check your surroundings before you take a single step. Look around you. Take your time."

Which was probably what Noah did every day of his life. That alertness that I'd come to realize was a part of him said he did and I was sure it was as natural to him as breathing. I vowed to be as like him as possible on the other side of the portal.

I tied the rope to my waist, took the leash from

Noah, and Midnight and I stepped through the portal. We found ourselves in a place that was not Earth. It was exactly as Noah had said. Large shade trees. Flowers of all colors, sizes, and shapes. An ocean not far away but too far for this first trip.

Everything grew thick and pressed in close, preventing me from seeing very far into the greenery that was everywhere. Only the ocean could be seen clearly and only because one of the huge trees blocking the view had fallen and the new growth hadn't yet grown tall enough to hide it from view.

Having satisfied myself that the ocean looked like a normal ocean, I moved my examination to the near-by shrubbery. Noah had said to be alert to my surroundings and the dense foliage would be the most likely place for something – some weird but deadly animal – to be hiding as it decided whether or not I'd make a decent meal. Noah's sense of his surroundings might make such an examination unnecessary for him because he'd know intuitively if there was danger. The same wasn't true of me. So I looked. Then I looked again. And, as a precaution, I looked still again.

There was something in that foliage. But it didn't resemble an animal. It was silver and shiny. Metallic. So what was it? I waited for a good two minutes before moving closer because, if I didn't know what it was then I didn't know what it might do if I got close. If it was some strange other-world machine set to kill intruders. Which was what we were. Intruders.

Satisfied as well as I could be that the shiny object wasn't about to send lethal, pointy things my way, I moved closer. The rope was long enough to easily allow a good examination and more because it was positioned a mere few yards from the portal and a bit to one side.

When I got close enough to see what it was I almost laughed. The relief was that great. It was a safe, the kind anyone could purchase online or in a hardware store. The kind people bought to prevent burglars from stealing things of value. It even had a company logo on the front, along with a Made in the USA label.

It was behind such thick greenery that I wondered if it was deliberately hidden, like the portal itself. Thinking that might be the case, I started to push through the greenery in front of it. And found that the greenery was fake, just like the shrubbery hiding the portal. Someone had deliberately hidden the safe.

So what was in it? Who had put it there and gone to considerable effort to hide it? More to the point, was it locked? I pushed aside the fake green stuff and tried to open the safe and found that it was, indeed, locked. And I stared at it for a long time, wondering who had put it there, how they'd done so, and why. Most of all, I wondered about the 'why.' What was its purpose?

I felt a tug on the rope and checked the time. Five minutes had elapsed. It was time for me to return to the real world. To Earth. So Midnight and I stepped back through the portal. But as the familiar territory of

Wyoming once again came into view I was glad I'd copied Noah's heightened awareness of his surroundings because that careful examination of the strange world beyond the portal had led to discovering the safe.

CHAPTER 5

I told Noah about the safe. He whistled silently and asked questions but there wasn't much to say. "We need to find the key," was his final evaluation.

"Do you think Uncle Cantrell put the safe there?"

He blew his breath out slowly. "I'm glad you said it first because I was wondering how to bring up the subject of your uncle without sounding judgmental."

" He'd be the most likely person to have the key as well as to be the person who hid both the portal and the safe."

"The portal is on his property." His look skewered me. "Your property now."

"If he had a key it should be somewhere in his cabin." I thought back to the property my family now owned. "He was a neat person so it shouldn't be hard to find if he had it."

"Except it appears he had a propensity to hide things. Like portals to other worlds."

"If it exists, I'll find it."

"Want some help?"

Hours of daylight stretched ahead but who knew how long it would take to find the key. If it existed. And if the search went into evening there were only kerosene lamps instead of electric ones, my uncle's way to conserve fuel for the generator. But if we left immediately the two of us could go through the cabin and hopefully conclude our search while the sun was still high. "Yes. Please help."

We secured the artificial shrubbery hiding the portal and brushed away our tracks with branches in case someone came by before heading back to Noah's ranch after which I drove to my new home, followed by Noah in his truck. I knew the way. How often would I make that same trip? Many times.

I couldn't wait to get back to the cabin and find the key – literally – that might unlock all kinds of secrets. In a moment that made me feel foolish, I was glad I'd made the bed that morning so Noah would think I was actually neat, which I wasn't.

I'd been in such a hurry I'd almost ignored the irritating task but a mother with a fetish for neat bedrooms had made me incapable of leaving it unmade. Uncle Cantrell had also been a neat freak, neat and tidy, and I hadn't been at the cabin long enough to turn it into my usual mess so it was impeccable. And that would make it easy to search.

The sun said it wasn't yet noon when I coasted to a stop next to the porch and shut off the engine. My emotions said it should have risen and set numerous times since leaving that morning. That much had happened since I was last on that porch.

"It's warm in here." Noah checked the wood stove. No glowing embers from last night but the stove wasn't cold. "It'll make searching more comfortable."

We looked around. A bedroom, the main room, a tiny bathroom, and a cubbyhole that must have started out as a pantry and ended up holding everything a bachelor would want to keep nearby. "I'll start in the bedroom."

Noah nodded. "I'll take the pantry. Whoever finishes first gets going on the main room."

"We're looking for a key. A small item." Our looks met as we acknowledged the difficulty of finding a key.

Even though the cabin wasn't large, every inch of wall and floor space held something. Clothes. Pots and pans. Several rifles that, according to Noah, were used for near, medium and long-range targets. Buckets. Firewood. Drawers of silverware, including razor-sharp knives of all sizes. Rope. Cowboy hats. And so on. Noah sighed. "It's going to be a long day."

We covered every inch of the bedroom and pantry. We took our time because we didn't want to miss anything and when we finished we could say with certainty that there was no key in either of them. Then we started on the main room.

Five minutes into our search Noah said, "It's getting too dark to see anything as small as a key." He was right. The sun was dipping below the horizon. We'd been working steadily for hours and found nothing and the kerosene lanterns wouldn't provide enough light. "I should get home."

I thought about it. "Can you stay here overnight?"

"I have to take care of the horses."

"I thought they were in the corral." He nodded. "Don't they have feed and water? Must they be inside at night?"

"Not necessarily. It's summer and Midnight wanted to stay with them." The huge dog had let us know in no uncertain terms that he wasn't coming with us. Noah's place had been his home for a while and he hadn't yet connected me with his real home. With Uncle Cantrell's place. So he disappeared when I started the car and called to him. "They'll be all right outside for one night with Midnight as a guard dog." He looked towards the wood stove. "Want me to get a fire going while you figure out what's for dinner?"

I wasn't the neatest housekeeper but coming from a family of bakers and cooks I knew how to throw together a meal and I did just that with the ease of much practice. Uncle Cantrell's pantry and storehouse had proved to be stocked with everything a hungry man could wish for.

Noah watched in admiration as I seared steaks, fried potatoes, and heated an assortment of frozen vegetables because they were all mixed together in one container in the freezer. "I'm the oldest of five kids and my parents often worked late so I know how to cook.”

“An excellent skill that I suspect I’m going to be grateful for very shortly.” He found dinnerware on homemade wooden shelves similar to the ones in his cabin and set the table. In no time we were eating and in less time then it took him to get things ready we were finished. I stared in surprise at my empty plate and wondered what it was about Wyoming that increased my appetite a hundred fold.

“I’ll sleep on the couch,” he said as he wiped the last of the dishes and put it away.

“You’re too tall.”

“It’s a long couch,” he replied and I looked and discovered he was right. The couch was homemade and longer than most. “Cantrell made it for sitting but also for overnight company. I’ve slept on it more than once.” He shook his head slowly. “And every time I slept there I wondered about his secret because I always thought he had one. Every time he dumped a pile of pillows and blankets on it for me to be comfortable there was something about his expression that said so.”

A light went off in my head. “You said he made it himself?” Noah nodded. “And you got that feeling when you were about to use the couch because of his expression at that moment?” He nodded again.

“Of course!” Our faces lit up. “The couch. He built a hiding place in the couch. That must be it.” Soon we were all over the couch, looking for a hiding place. “It’ll be small and will look like it’s part of the overall construction so no one who doesn't know about it will be suspicious."

But we knew. Even so, we went over the couch three times before finding a board that wasn't essential to the construction of the couch on one end and then we still weren't sure it was the right place because there was a similar board on the other end.

"He'd have made both ends alike so no one would be suspicious. But one of them will be fake and the other will be the hiding place." Noah looked at me. We were on our knees, inches apart with the couch tipped on its side as we felt every inch of it. Even in the dim light of the kerosene lamp I could see excitement in his eyes.

Blue. They were a shade of blue that matched a stormy sky. They were lit up and eager. "Which end is the hiding place?" Because one of them must be.

We felt around the boards at each end of the couch. "This one," he said triumphantly as he felt behind the board and found a latch. He turned the latch and a small cavity appeared. In the cavity was the kind of key that was used to open safes. He held it high. "We found it."

We put the key back where it had been hidden. No better place to keep it overnight but we were too excited to go to sleep immediately so we sat up long into the night drinking black coffee and eating cookies I'd brought all the way from the family bakery in Illinois until we ran out of things to say and sheer exhaustion took over.

As I slid into my bed I wondered briefly if I was a fool to trust a man I hardly knew with the key that would unlock whatever my uncle had hidden that must have been meant for my family.

Then I remembered those stormy blue eyes and easy smile and decided to trust Noah. Maybe I was foolish but after the day we'd shared and the things we'd discovered, we were already past the beginning stages of friendship.

Maybe nothing had been said but I felt that friendship in every fiber of my being. Besides, I told myself as I dropped into a dreamless sleep, he might be sleeping next to the key to the safe but I had the keys to my car and I'd hear if he went anywhere in his truck. It was that old and that loud.

Noah turned out to be a morning person. The smell of frying bacon and the sound of tuneless humming woke me before the sun rose. I turned over, pulled the blanket over my head, then pushed it away and got up because no one could sleep with two such invasive things pushing sleep away at the precise moment the sun came up.

The tuneless hum turned into a song loud enough to wake a deaf person and I yelled that I was awake so he could stop now. He did and I thought I heard a muffled laugh that I ignored as I tried to make myself presentable as best as I could with the only sink in the cabin being in the kitchen where he was making breakfast.

I used the rudimentary bathroom, wished it had a sink so I'd not have to use the shower for water but eventually I was thoroughly awake and glad for the warmth of the wood stove. "I'm done with the sink if you want to clean up," was all he said as he examined me shivering. "Or do you want to warm up first?" He moved away from the stove.

"Both." But breakfast was ready so I cleaned up after we did the dishes and put everything away. There were no horses here so no chores for him to do so he sat on that long couch with the bedding already put away and put his long legs on a stool and watched without comment as I washed my hair and pulled it into a pony tail.

Then he said, "Do you always wear your hair like that?"

"When I'm going to be out in the wind and who knows what kind of weather in another world."

"Just wondered because if long hair is a problem I'd think you'd get it cut short." I shook my head to dry it somewhat and he said, sotto voice, "It would dry faster if it was loose." He was right. I loosened it and he nodded approval. "Looks nice that way. It'll dry fast enough in the car. You can tie it up again when we get the horses and head for the portal."

The horses were waiting for their morning treats and were ready and eager to go somewhere. The pack horse was laden when we left the corral with Midnight running ahead sometimes and other times behind and generally everywhere, coming back to us often to make sure we were still okay. The day was bright and I was humming with anticipation. I wished I could run alongside him and get rid of some of the energy that made the ride seem to take both too much time while at the same time not enough.

Then we reached the rock formation and the portal. It was time to find out what was in the safe. We stared at the brush hiding the portal for a time before removing it. It was that important and we needed a moment to absorb the implications of our next move.

"Midnight doesn't have to come this time. He can do his exploring in the world he knows best."

I agreed. Then Noah gave me a look I couldn't read and took my hand. And we went through.

CHAPTER 6

It was exactly as before. An ocean not far away, with waves washing onto a white sand beach. Jungle-like growth everywhere but with a balmy, comfortable temperature. Not a cloud in sight. If this world had clouds. Maybe it didn't. And a rope anchored in our own world because we weren't taking any chances. It looked like paradise but looks can be deceiving.

We checked the new world out, scanning from one side to the other to see as much as possible from where we stood. Then we went straight to the safe hidden behind and beneath more artificial greenery. But there was enough bright metal to see it if we knew what to look for.

We pulled the greenery off the safe with ease. By then we were practiced at removing it, having done the same thing with the artificial greenery concealing the portal itself. We carefully placed it to one side. Then I knelt before the safe and started to insert the key.

"Wait." Noah's hand stopped mine. "Let me do it."

I gave him a startled look. "Why?"

His eyes went all hooded. He didn't want me reading his thoughts. "Just let me do it, okay?"

Was this some macho thing? The big guy wants to open the safe that might contain a king's ransom worth of jewels? But it wasn't worth arguing about. I handed him the key.

He inserted the key and turned it. We both heard a click. "Stand away," he said tersely, gesturing me away with one hand while the other rested on the door of the safe.

It wasn't a macho thing after all. He was afraid the safe was rigged and would blow up when the door swung open. He was taking the risk. Protecting me. I wanted to shove past him and do the opening myself because this was a joint effort and I should take as many risks as he did. But it was too late. He pulled the door open.

And nothing happened. If I hadn't figured out that he feared the safe was rigged I'd not have noticed the slight release of tension in his shoulders because I'd not have noticed that tension to begin with. But I had figured it out so I did see his body relax and knew why he took a long, deep breath.

"There's something inside." He reached in and pulled out a cloth bag, the kind jewelry is often kept in. He didn't open it. Instead he handed it to me.

I took it and made sure our looks collided. "I'm surprised you're letting me open it. It might go 'bang.'"

He shrank. "Sorry. It was a habit."

"What? Protecting the little, frail, helpless female?"

His eyes went wide. His mouth dropped open. Then he laughed loudly. "You? Frail? Helpless? Really?" And he laughed some more. "You came a thousand miles alone to a place with no power and lots of rattlesnakes and then insisted on coming through an impossible portal to a world that can't exist but does. If you really think I consider you a frail, helpless female you've got another think coming."

"But you insisted on opening the safe."

He flushed. He'd been so self-assured up to that moment that I loved that he could be flustered but he continued as if he hoped I didn't notice. "It came naturally. I'm bossy. Besides, I've been around more than you have."

I wondered just what that meant. What kind of life had he lived? But I forgot to think further because he wasn't finished. "Believe me when I say that the next time I think danger is possible, I'll step back and let you handle it. Maybe I'll even give you a shove in the direction of the danger." But his slight embarrassment at being caught out in a protective gesture was slow to disappear and I liked that about him.

He was kneeling beside the safe. I dropped to the ground near him, pulled the drawstring open and felt inside the cloth bag. "It's some kind of stones." I pulled out a couple. There were more in the bag but they all felt similar.

"Jewels?" They were pendant shaped, multi-colored, smooth as glass and had inscriptions carved into the surface. "There's a hole for a cord. Necklaces?"

"What do the inscriptions say?" I gave Noah one of the stones so we could each examine one but they appeared identical.

"I don't know. It's not English." He turned the over stone in his hand several times. "I don't recognize the writing. It doesn't look like its Middle Eastern or Oriental or anything I've ever seen." He looked at mine. "What about yours?"

"The same. I have no idea what language the writing is."

He placed his stone in my hand next to the one I already held. They were exactly the same, down to identical inscriptions. "What about the rest of the stones?"

I took off my sweater and set it on the ground. Then I dumped all of the stones from the bag onto it. We spread them neatly on the sweater and added the ones we each held. They were all identical.

We looked at them for a while, turning them over, making sure there were no differences. "Why so many?"

"Enough to go around if there are several people wanting them?"

We counted them. "Sixteen stones. Not a number that makes any kind of sense."

I examined the stones further. "My mother has a pair of opal earrings. They look like these stones." Many colors with a depth that seemed to go on forever. They could be opals."

"And they are sort of oval with holes in them. So they could be jewelry. Earrings or necklaces."

"Or the hole could be to make it easy to carry them. A cord through the hole would make it easy to tie the cord to anything so it doesn't get lost."

"The writing doesn't make sense if they are jewelry."

"Some jewelry has sentimental verses."

Noah rocked back on his heels. "I wonder if we'll ever know."

I placed the stones back in their bag and put the bag in my backpack and then looked at him. "Now what?"

His eyes lit up. "How about a little exploring?" He looked longingly at the ocean lapping on the nearby beach.

"We didn't bring enough rope." We were still tethered to the rope that was secured to a stake in the ground in our world and it wouldn't reach the ocean. Rather I was tethered. Since we only had one rope, Noah wasn't tied to anything.

He gave me a look. He was dying to do something in this other world. Anything. "Just to the beach."

"Don't do anything stupid."

The look I got after that remark said volumes.

"Nothing stupid. I promise."

I'd only known him a few days but that was enough to know the man before me was anything but stupid and would never take unnecessary chances. Plus he'd see more in one glance than I'd see in an hour. In the meantime, I was tied to a tether. He wasn't. "Go. Check out the beach. See if it's like any beaches in our world. Take pictures."

He kept his word and was back quickly. "It's beautiful. A veritable paradise. When we're more comfortable with this whole portal business we must go swimming and have a bonfire on the beach. It's pure white sand and feels like a carpet. It goes for miles. We could run along the shore almost forever."

I looked longingly at the ocean with its lovely beach. "We have what we came for. We should go."

He sighed. "Midnight is probably antsy by now and thinks we deserted him."

We gathered our few things and headed for the portal. Moments later we walked through as if going through a doorway from one room to another. It was that easy. The sun said less than an hour had passed since we entered the other world but Midnight was all over us with relief that he hadn't been abandoned.

I slid my backpack to the ground and grabbed one of the last of the stale cookies from Noah's place and gave it to him. He slobbered all over me with love and thanks and swallowed it in one gulp. Then he left to continue exploring the area.

The day stretched ahead but seemed anticlimactic. We had the stones but had no idea what they were made of or how they were important. We didn't know if they were important at all other than they'd been under lock and key. We stared at one another. What to do next?

As we stared, the sun that had promised heat as soon as it rose high enough kept that promise. It was not only bright, it was growing truly hot. The surrounding area was covered with brush but few trees grew there and those were farther away than I felt like walking. But as the sun began to slant to the west the rock formation itself began to provide shade. A sliver at first but as the hours passed it would be quite comfortable and the formation itself could be used as a back rest.

I headed for that small streak of shade and Noah followed but the prickly shrubbery proved too uncomfortable to lean against. Noah muttered under his breath and began tearing it away from the rock face. Then he stopped and took a deep breath.

"More artificial shrubbery."

I whirled around. Sure enough, the prickly brush that had made leaning against it uncomfortable was identical to what had hidden the portal and both appeared real and blended in with the natural bushes around us. Uncle Cantrell must have gone to a lot of trouble to find just the right artificial green stuff.

"Why here? Another portal?"

But as we pulled this new shrub away from the

rock face no door shape jumped out at us. But something did. Something unnatural.

"It's writing. It's like a page out of a book."

"Like the writing on the stones."

A large rectangular space on the face of the rock was as flat and smooth as a piece of paper. On that space were markings similar to the markings on the stones. They were in regular rows or columns. It was impossible to tell which because the entire page – and it so resembled a page out of a book that we thought of it that way – had symbols arranged so precisely that they could be read either up and down like a column of numbers or side to side like sentences in a book. And we had no idea which they were or what they meant.

I took one of the stones from my backpack and the similarity was undeniable. "They are pieces of the same puzzle. The stones in that other world and whatever this writing is in our world."

"We need a cryptographer."

"We're in the middle of the Wyoming back country."

"There's a library in town." The small town I'd stopped in to make one last call to my family.

"I doubt they'll have much in such a small library about hieroglyphics."

"They might. People in this part of the west are proud of the Native pictographs."

"It's as good a place as any to start our search."

"We need to know what these marks say."

"What they say could decide whether we enjoy that swim in the ocean and bonfire on the beach or stay away from whatever monsters are waiting to eat us alive."

"By the time we get back to the cabin and head for town the library will be closed."

"Tomorrow."

So once again we had to wait. The miles that separated places on the map also separated them by time. I decided patience mut be a virtue learned young by the natives of this state. And Noah's expression said it was normal to space the segments of any project over many days. "I'll stop by your place early so we can be in town as soon as the library opens. Be waiting."

"I'll have breakfast if you want."

"Sounds good. I'll be there at dawn."

Of course he would. If he arrived that early, by the time we'd eaten, cleared the table, and driven to town, early morning would have come and gone and the library would be open.

"Let's take pictures of the carvings before we leave so we can compare them to whatever we find in books." So we snapped pictures of every single symbol, making sure to note where on the rock page each was located.

We'd put the pictures together when we reached my cabin and could print them out. The generator provided enough electricity for minimal electronics and a computer and printer had been in the cabin when I arrived.

The printed pages would create a replica of the rock page that we could compare to what we found in the library. We'd crack the code. We'd know what it was trying to tell us.

CHAPTER 7

Decoding the rock carvings turned out to be more problematic than expected. The library had an extensive section on local pictographs because there were a lot of them and everyone, locals and visitors alike, wanted to learn about them. They were fascinating, informative, Indigenous, and filled an entire room dedicated to local history and we had the room to ourselves while we compared pictographs to carvings.

None matched. "Not even close."

We'd gone through more books than I'd have believed existed on the arcane subject of ancient writings in North America. We'd looked twice. Checked the main room just in case some books hadn't been transferred to this special room. And we'd found nothing even closely resembling the put-together picture laid out on the rather large library table in the center of the room for people like us. Seekers of knowledge.

Noah's shoulders visibly drooped in disappointment. "Maybe there are more? These are local. Maybe pictographs from other areas will be similar to the carvings."

"We can ask." The way those shoulders remained slumped said he wasn't hopeful.

The librarian wasn't hopeful either. She examined our taped together collage of carving pictures for a long time before shaking her head. "I don't recognize them."

She peered at us over a pair of reading glasses that were the perfect complement to the blonde bun and long, floaty dress she hoped made her appear much older than her twenty-something years as she continued. "And I majored in Indigenous pictographs."

She grinned suddenly, wrecking her every effort to appear seriously academic. "That major is why I got this job and I love it here." She leaned over the counter, shoving a dozen books aside to make enough space. "This town is kind of known for ancient languages."

She pulled back and tried to regain her beloved-old-professor appearance. "It's because of Ralph Williams, of course." She meticulously replaced the books she'd scattered. "Because he decided to retire here. And, of course the reason he retired here was because of the many pictographs in the area."

"Who's Ralph Williams?"

She blinked in surprise at our lack of local knowledge. "You don't know? You've never heard of the famous Ralph Williams? Cryptographer extraordinaire."

Noah and I exchanged looks and came to the same conclusion. We wanted to talk with this person. "Where does he live? Do you know?"

Noah added, "Do you think he'll look at these carvings?"

"He'd be insulted if you don't contact him.

Decoding old writings is his passion as well as having been the job that paid his bills for many years."

She told us where to find him. Not an address because they weren't used in such a small place. "Do you think he'll be home?"

"It's a small town. If he isn't home he'll most likely be in the cafe."

It was a tiny town. Barely more than a hamlet. It wasn't even incorporated. As we exited the library I suspected this former college professor was the reason Whitehall had a library and was definitely the reason its collection of Indigenous pictographs had its own room.

The important thing, though, was that we were about to become the fortunate recipients of all those years of accumulated knowledge. If he agreed to examine our pictures.

We found him easily in the only café in town. The waitress who was also the cook and probably the owner of the café nodded towards an elderly man in a booth overlooking the street. "He likes to people watch so he always takes that booth."

People watch? The street was deserted. But perhaps that wasn't always the case. It was possible that a handful of people would meander through town and you could see them all if you sat in that booth long enough.

There was a book open beside the coffee that he was likely lingering over after having finished lunch. I suspected he'd spend the whole afternoon in that booth watching people and reading. From his contented expression I thought he'd chosen his retirement option well.

There was an air of intellectual curiosity in the way

he looked at both book and the world beyond the window. It wasn't exactly the same aura of alertness that was a part of Noah, but as I watched I suspected it came from a similar personality trait. Both lived life fully and wanted to be aware of everything around them. Physically for Noah and intellectually for Ralph Williams. It was part of who and what they were. I decided Ralph Williams was an older, wiser and much milder version of Noah.

He was exactly what we needed and I knew even before we approached him that he'd help with our quest. As we grew close he figured out that we were there to see him and he shoved his book aside and we slid into the booth across from him. "May I help you?" Without giving us a chance to answer, he continued. "You're here about local cave paintings aren't you?"

We looked at each other, then at him and Noah said, "Not exactly." The elderly man's eyebrows rose in question. "Inscriptions on a rock formation on Emma's property. Carvings, not paintings."

He considered Noah's words. "Interesting. Unusual. Can you describe them?" He didn't ask if we wanted his expertise because obviously that was why we were here, which meant the man before us was used to being consulted.

I pulled the patched together pictures of the carvings and showed them to him. They were so extensive I had to fold the paper several times to fit on the booth table but enough of the carvings showed to be a representative sample.

He examined them and his expression changed from polite and helpful to carefully concealed excitement. "I don't recognize them." He examined the entire patchwork of pictures. "Would it be possible for me to see all the carvings?"

Noah stood up to comply but Ralph Williams indicated he shouldn't unfold the rather large put-together picture. "Not here. My house is nearby." Of course it was nearby in such a tiny hamlet where everything was nearby. "Will you come with me?"

He shoved the coffee aside and gathered his book. Then he led us out of the café and down a side street to a smallish, neat house that, like most houses in Whitehall, wasn't locked.

The dining room was the largest room in the house and was almost completely taken up by a large table with books that looked like they belonged in a college library and probably did. He cleared the table and Noah spread the pasted-together image of the carvings on the table. It took up almost the entire space.

"Oh my goodness," was the first thing Ralph Williams said, followed by, "Is the carved area as large as it appears to be?" We said the carvings were slightly larger in real life. He sucked in a breath that could have meant anything or nothing.

He bent closely over the pictures and examined them carefully for a long time. Then he stood upright and said, "I've never seen this writing before. Nothing even close."

He acted as though he thought the whole thing was a hoax. Noah and I exchanged glances. We had to do something to make this expert a believer.

"The carvings are real." Ralph Williams leaned back a bit and dared Noah to prove the truth of his claim. "What can we do to prove it to you?"

"Is that rock formation nearby?"

We looked at each other. We couldn't take him to the rock formation. He might learn of the existence of the portal. But before we could think what to say, Ralph said, "I'll check out a few things this evening. I'm sure I've never seen this particular language before but there might be something similar. Something close enough to know where to start."

"Then will you be able to read the carvings?"

Ralph smiled widely. Proudly. "It's what I do. It's my favorite thing. Decoding encrypted messages is an art form and ancient languages never come with a secret decoding device but I'm good at what I do. So if the carvings are genuine then I'm certain I'm up to the challenge and I'll be reading them sooner rather than later." Then he added, "They look genuine in the pictures but of course there's no way to know for sure without seeing the carving themselves."

"We'll appreciate anything you can do."

"I'll see what I can come up with. Next time you're in town stop by and maybe I'll have something."

We left the pictures with him. We could take more. Then we left and drove to my home. Noah hung around to play with Midnight but talk turned to the next day's events. "I hope we're doing the right thing showing those pictures to Ralph Williams."

We were on the porch but there was only one chair, a rocking chair, so we dropped to the steps and threw balls for Midnight to chase. It was warm, just the right temperature, and the sun was a red ball in the sky as it dropped towards night. We sat a long time and the longer we sat the more acutely I became aware of the man beside me.

What was it about him that set my body

thrumming? His acute awareness of his surroundings that I'd never seen in anyone before? Or his sculpted, outdoor type body? I didn't know whether I wished him to move farther away or closer. Whether I wanted the feeling to grow or disappear. But we were there for a purpose so I forced myself back to the topic of Ralph Williams.

"What choice did we have? He's the expert if we want to find out what they say."

"It's your property. Who knows what will happen if this whole thing turns out to be monumental in some way?" The sun dropped behind the horizon with a swiftness that startled me and suddenly it wasn't evening any more, it was a soft, warm, almost fuzzy night. "Who knows what will happen to your lovely, secluded ranch."

"What we found is already monumental."

Noah nodded, sighed, and rose. "It's getting late. I'd best get home if we're going to get an early start." We'd agreed to meet at his place sometime after breakfast and Noah promised to have the horses ready. We'd not even considered not going to the portal. Not considered taking a break. We literally couldn't stay away.

The warmth I'd thought was the night dissipated as he rose and I realized it was my proximity to the man that had warmed me. Hey, girl, I told myself as I watched him climb into his truck and disappear in the dark, be careful because this is about strange carvings on rocks and strange, other worlds and about the portal that links those things together. It's not about Noah and how he makes you feel.

Except, as I headed inside to dinner and sleep, I

reminded myself that Noah was a big part of this endeavor. Half or more. He had the horses that could get us to the rock formation through terrain that would destroy the undercarriage of my tiny car and I already knew I wanted him as a partner while exploring the world beyond the portal. I needed the strength and skills that he'd acquired from years in the Wyoming back country while I'd lived in a comfortable Midwestern home. I needed him. So I sternly told myself to forget my feelings and concentrate on that other world.

Though it was entirely possible that now it wouldn't be just the two of us. Ralph Williams could very well become a third member of what I now thought of as a team. It could happen if he did what we'd asked him to do. If he deciphered the carvings and if, through reading them, learned of the existence of the portal.

CHAPTER 8

The next day, after eating, Midnight and I headed to Noah's place. We'd decided not to bring him to the portal because we didn't know him well enough to take him to another world. We didn't know what we'd do in another world so definitely didn't know how a dog would react.

Since he was familiar with Noah's place, he'd stay there while we went exploring and, sure enough, his ears pricked up when he realized where we were going and he jumped out the instant I opened the door and then he set about checking the whole place to learn what had happened since he'd been there last.

"I'm bringing a couple guns," Noah said without preamble when I reached the porch. "You have a thing about guns?"

"I'm good but will they work in the other world?"

His eyes went dark. "Even though it kind of resembles our world, it's different. Maybe things work differently there." He went into his cabin and reappeared with two rifles and a pistol in a holster strapped around his waist.

"We'll find out if they work soon enough." He

came close and strapped a second holster around my waist. The weight was both scary and satisfying. "Now we'll be ready. If guns work there. We'll check. And electronics."

"Why electronics?"

"The cell phone took pictures. Today I have walkie-talkies. All are electronic. Cell phones don't work around here unless they are satellite phones so I have walkie-talkies that are the newest and best so hopefully we can use them to communicate between worlds. It'll be wonderful if they work through the portal."

Midnight came running to us, ears up and alert. "What's with Midnight?"

"Don't have a clue but he's excited about something."

"Is he a hunting dog?"

"I don't know. Cantrell never said anything about it, but he does see the guns."

"He's acting like our neighbor's dog back in Illinois. The neighbor went duck hunting every autumn and the dog was a trained retriever that went crazy the moment the duck decoys and guns were brought out because he knew it meant a hunting trip was in the future. He loved those trips."

Noah leaned the rifles against the porch and Midnight's tail wagged furiously. "Evidently he likes to hunt." Noah shook his head. "I never knew."

"Or maybe Uncle Cantrell took him to the other world. Maybe they went hunting there." Or for the same reason we were taking guns with us. "Or perhaps Uncle Cantrell took guns for protection and took Midnight for the same reason."

"Could be." We watched Midnight's antics. "But I'm still not comfortable taking him today. We'll go through but we won't stick close to the portal. We've not left the immediate area of the portal before. It's too risky to take Midnight. He's a good dog but we don't know what he'll do. I don't want to lose him."

Midnight let us know how insulted he was when we left him behind but, being a good and obedient dog, he didn't try to follow, just barked loudly as we left the corral and headed for the rock formation.

If we didn't know the portal was there we wouldn't have found it. We'd done that good of a job of concealing it behind the fake greenery Uncle Cantrell had used. We removed it carefully so as to keep it looking like a real bush and anchored it against the fake green stuff that hid the carvings. Then we tied the horses nearby with water and a little grain. Then we looked at one another. We were ready.

"The guns and walkie-talkies. We go through and test them immediately so if they don't work we can leave them behind. They are heavy. No sense carrying them if they are useless."

The guns and walkie-talkies worked very well in the other world. After a bit of experimentation we learned the walkie-talkies also worked between worlds. So we filled our holsters with ammunition for the pistols, put more in our pockets for the rifles, slung the walkie-talkies around our necks, and proceeded to enter the other world.

We got as far as that white sand beach beside the azure blue ocean. The scene was so beautiful, so peaceful, so idyllic, that we simply sat down and soaked up the ambience. We turned our faces to the dull red sun that poured heat down on us even though it didn't have the brilliance of our own sun. We leaned the rifles against a log on the edge of the beach and removed our holsters, though we kept them nearby. Just in case.

"Keep them close enough to grab if something comes from the forest and charges us." Noah was torn between wearing that holster and enjoying the sand beach. "The beach gives enough distance that nothing can sneak up on us but if something comes at us really fast we'll have to act faster."

"It seems so peaceful and we've been here a couple times already. I can't believe something terrible will charge us."

"Stay alert."

But I relaxed because I knew Noah's natural alertness would be on watch. He didn't know how not to be alert. The knowledge was comforting as I walked to the ocean and removed my boots and stuck a toe in the water. "It's perfect. Not too hot, not too cold." And the sound of waves lapping on the shore was hypnotic.

Noah heaved a sigh of defeat and followed my example and soon we were wading in the lukewarm water. But I noticed that even though he enjoyed wading as much as I did, he was constantly watching the undergrowth, eyes moving back and forth as he smiled and kicked water my way and generally acted like a kid on a school outing.

Then his face darkened. "Get out of the water. Fast!" Before the words were said he was grabbing my arm and dragging me onto the beach and didn't stop until we were beside our weapons and in seconds one of those rifles was in his arms and aimed at the ocean.

"I hope they are like ocean creatures we know of but if they aren't – if they come out of the water – they'll get a loud and deadly welcome." A rifle was at his shoulder but he didn't pull the trigger. He just watched.

I followed his look and saw several large shadows not far from where we'd been wading. Too large to come into the shallow water but not very far out. They didn't come closer. Instead they swam back and forth, looking our way and trying to get closer but eventually they gave up and disappeared back in the ocean from which they'd come.

Noah set the rifle back down and we dropped once more to the sand. "They might not have been dangerous."

"Or they might have eaten us alive." What might have happened if Noah hadn't been watchful made me actually tremble. I tried to hide it and failed. I was that shook up. "Thank you for possibly saving my life."

"No problem. I'm sure you'll do the same for me some day." He moved closer and pulled me close, pretty much like an adult would do with a frightened child. I pulled away and straightened and made the trembling stop. I wasn't a child and I most assuredly didn't want Noah to think of me as one. He dropped his hands. "Sorry. I didn't mean anything."

Our looks met. His was apologetic. Mine was confused. "Nothing to apologize for. But you don't have to comfort me every time I sneeze. I want to deal with things on my own because I want to be comfortable in this beautiful unknown world."

"Too comfortable could be dangerous."

He was right. "Okay. In that case, you can comfort

me all you want."

Instead of gathering me back in his arms, which wasn't needed because I was obviously not in need of more comfort but the lack of his arms around me left me feeling kind of empty, he said, "It's best if we don't stray far from the portal today. Maybe we should just sit here on the beach and see what happens. If anything else swims by. Or comes out of the forest for a visit and decides to eat us."

"It's a lovely beach. I can happily sit here all day."

"But no more swimming. Let's not tempt fate."

Conversation lapsed. Silence surrounded us, but it wasn't true silence. I was lulled by the sound of lapping waves creeping almost to where our feet stretched out on the sand and by the whisper of wind in the trees beyond the beach. And more sounds I didn't recognize.

I sat up, suddenly alert, and looked to Noah. What did he think of those sounds? Was my hyper-vigilant companion listening? Of course he was. His head was tipped back and his body was turned just enough to see both the beach and forest and there was something about him that, now that I knew there were sounds coming from that forest, told me that he, also, heard them. And had said nothing.

I confronted him. "Do you hear those sounds?"

"Yep." His eyes slitted.

"They could be dangerous." Like the ocean creatures could have been.

"Probably not." He didn't move. Not an inch. "But maybe they are."

"Should we leave?"

"Not yet."

He turned towards me and smiled. Reassuringly.

Gently. He was both gentle and tough as nails at the same time. The man was a mystery but that smile settled my insides. Not that he knew any more than I did but two people felt somehow safer than one, especially if Noah was one of those people.

Had Uncle Cantrell been afraid? How had he handled fear? But whatever was in that forest, Uncle Cantrell had come back enough times to warrant leaving a safe here. Surely that meant something about the safety of the place.

Then the sounds faded as whatever had made them moved away. Noah leaned back and gave a sigh of relief that said more than words how concerned he'd been. Next time I'd not believe his glib reassurances. I'd watch his eyes instead and know whether I should panic.

The odd sun moved across the sky. "A day here must be about the same as in our world."

We ate the jerky we'd brought, and the apples and the chocolate candy. And we sat on that beach until it lost its appeal but the ocean mere yards away looked bluer and bluer and more and more inviting and whatever monsters had tried to attack us were gone.

"I'm going wading again."

Noah looked at me. Held my gaze. Dropped his when he realized no lecture from him would stop me from doing what I wanted to do. He nodded. "Might as well. It's kind of what we're here for. Sitting in fear won't teach us much about this place." He rose in one easy movement. "But you do the wading. I'll keep watch."

"We can take turns."

So we did. A few minutes each, with one of us

scanning the ocean while the other waded and kicked water onto the beach. But nothing disturbed the afternoon and eventually that foreign sun said it was time to leave because it was dropping towards that alien horizon. If this world was like ours, different creatures would stalk the night. More dangerous ones.

We gathered our equipment and headed towards the portal. It was an anticlimax because other than two shadows in the water we'd not seen a thing to give us a clue what this other world was like.

"It'll probably take many trips," Noah said, echoing my thought.

"I have the time if you do." He nodded. He'd not said how much time he normally spent earning a living but whatever he did clearly didn't require a fixed schedule.

"I wonder if Ralph Williams has decoded anything yet."

"That's next on our list. After we get a better idea what this world is like."

"So we come back here tomorrow?"

"And the day after that. And the day after that. And so on. Until we feel safe venturing far from the portal."

"And then we visit Ralph Williams again."

CHAPTER 9

Days in the other world must have been shorter than in ours because when we emerged through the portal our own, a bright sun still hung high in the sky. It was midafternoon.

"We have time to take more pictures of the carvings. That way Ralph Williams can have one set and we'll have another. Maybe we, too, can do some decoding."

So we pushed the artificial brush away from the carvings. "Let's include the stones in the pictures since they have the same symbols." I pulled one of the stones from the bag and held it next to the carvings while Noah snapped pictures and finally said, "That should be enough."

With the stone in my hand, I bent over to retrieve the bag that I'd dropped to the ground next to the carvings. In so doing, I dropped the stone. It brushed against the rock formation, sliding across the symbols as it skipped its way to the ground.

As it went downward, everything began to glow.

Rock formation, falling stone, and carvings all took on a soft silver sheen.

"What the -- ?" Noah started towards me because I was so close that I, too, was enclosed by the glow. I must have scared him. "Are you okay?" Seeing I was unhurt, he asked, "What just happened?"

"The stone touched the carvings as it fell." I showed him the stone that was now on the ground. I picked it up. Covered it. Hid it from whatever unseen force had made it glow.

Noah examined me, the stones, and the rock formation behind me. "When the stone hit the ground it no longer touched the carvings and the glow ceased. Is that right? " I agreed and he asked again, "Are you sure you're okay?

I didn't hurt. I'd felt nothing. So whatever had happened hadn't been dangerous. I opened my hand to touch one of the stones to the carvings again because that was what had made everything glow but Noah saw what I was planning and put out a hand to stop me. But it would be safe. I somehow knew that.

I ignored his frown and touched the stone to the carvings a second time and once more everything glowed silver but this time I didn't pull the stone away. I moved it over the carvings and the glow held steady but as I slowed the movement and then stopped the glow in the rock formation faded but the carvings and the stone in my hand retained the same silver glow as before.

I held the stone against the carvings long enough to know it would keep glowing as long as they touched each other. Then I pulled it away and the glow disappeared. The world was once again as it had been before I dropped the stone.

Noah gestured towards the portal. "The stone, the portal, and the carvings. They are all connected. When the stone touched the carvings, it did something. Started something. Or changed something. It's the only rational explanation for what just happened."

I followed his look and his thoughts. "Nothing changed. Everything looks the same. It's as if nothing happened."

"Something changed. We just don't know what it was."

"Because the change is on the other side of the portal?"

"The only way to find out if that's what happened is to go back through and take a good look around."

We were in agreement. "So let's see if the other world changed."

Noah nodded. "But we must acknowledge that we know so little about the other world that we might not notice a subtle difference."

"We should look anyway."

We went to the portal. We held hands because this wasn't like the other times we'd gone through. This time was different because we knew something might have changed and we had no idea whether that change would be good or bad. We had no idea what waited on the other side. My stomach clenched. Then we stepped through and were almost blown off our feet by a howling blizzard.

It was so cold it hurt to breathe and the wind blew so hard that if we'd stayed even a minute we'd have gotten frostbite. Any longer and we'd have been in serious trouble.

We backed out immediately and watched the snow that now lay thick on our shoulders, hair and every other part of our anatomies melt in Wyoming's late afternoon heat. I said what we were both thinking. "That was scary."

"But informative."

"The other world changed from summer to winter."

"Or the world we stepped into wasn't the same world. Was a different world entirely. A winter world."

"When the stone touched the rock carvings it could have changed the portal to take us to a different world."

"How do we find out which it was?"

"We return dressed for the worst winter weather imaginable and check out that white and dangerous world. We see if we recognize anything about it. The ocean. The trees. Whatever."

"What if it's a different world where blizzards never stop?"

"Then we'll never go back again."

"How do we go somewhere else?"

"Obviously the stones change the world the portal opens onto. We'll figure it out because you and I both know we intend to explore what's beyond the portal and this makes me – and I suspect you – even more eager to become intrepid explorers."

The next day when we stepped through the portal, the snow storm was nowhere to be seen. Clothed in parkas over the warmest clothes we possessed while wearing clumsy snow boots we made sure Midnight and the horses were comfortable in the Wyoming morning before stepping into that winter world.

The blizzard had ended but the cold still took our breath away and a brutally bright sun that provided no warmth at all turned the new world so white that we were blinded. If we stayed too long we'd succumb to snow blindness. But we didn't stay. Just long enough to determine whether this was indeed a different world and that was quickly obvious.

There were no trees, no growing things of any kind, and where the ocean had been in the previous world steep cliffs stood in this one. Even if we wished to explore this frigid world, those cliffs made doing so impossible.

Noah was right that it was an entirely different world so we headed back to our own comfortable world where Midnight and the horses waited patiently and winter wouldn't come for many months. After minimal discussion we left them at Noah's ranch and headed to Whitehall to see if Ralph Williams had had a breakthrough and decoded the carvings. We now knew what purpose they served, changing the portal to a different world, but we didn't know how to make them do what we'd want them to do. Only Ralph could help us with that.

"It's only been a couple days since you gave me the pictures. Not enough time to do more than look them over." Seeing our disappointment he added, "But I did get a start. I can't read anything yet but I have some thoughts." We were standing at the doorway to his small house. He gestured for us to enter. "Come in and

I'll show you what I've figured so far."

The pasted together pictures still covered the dining room table but it now also held almost a dozen books that had previously been on the shelves that filled one side of the room, taking up the small amount of space the table didn't. Now there were gaps in those shelves where books had been removed. Two of them lay open.

"You figured out what language the carvings are written in?"

Ralph wagged his head as he considered the pictures. "Not a clue and I spent half a night and all day yesterday comparing your carvings to every written language I have access to. Nothing even came close." He put enough of the books on a chair to be able to once more see the entire picture of the carved portion of the rock formation. "But I do believe I've figured out one thing and that's a start."

There was nothing on the table except the pictures and books. No papers where he'd tried different codes. No notes. But he looked happy in a way I suspected he'd looked in his university office every time he'd had a breakthrough during his long career.

He pointed to the pictures. "I believe they are mostly numbers." He traced the carvings. "See how neatly they are arranged? Not in linear fashion as is usual with writing. Rather these are in precise columns similar to what we use when organizing numbers for some mathematical purpose."

He continued, "A few very ancient forms of writing are done in a similar manner. Cuneiform, for example. But even so, I think these are numbers. There are only a few of them that are repeated often and in most languages, there are fewer numerals than letters. So I think these are numbers."

It made sense. Touching numbers would have opened the portal and what numbers were touched and in what order they were chosen would decide what world it opened onto. I felt a rising excitement as I studied the pictures.

But Ralph wasn't finished. "But I believe a few of them might be letters."

He traced one of the carvings and saw things in them that made no sense to me but spoke volumes to him. "I believe these carvings to be a mix of both letters and numbers similar to what we might find on many items today. Product codes. Identification of some type. Except these aren't recent. They are ancient. I suspect they are extremely old because I can't find anything similar anywhere."

He looked at us over his glasses. "I'd truly like to see the rock formation itself. I can't promise that seeing it would enable me to read the symbols any better than looking at these pictures does. But there's always the chance it might help." His elderly gray eyes were sharp and piercing. "So what do you think? Will you take me there?"

Noah and I remained silent. We wanted to know how the carvings operated the portal. We needed to know how it worked if we were to explore with reasonable safety whatever worlds were beyond the portal. But it was a secret so monumental and with implications beyond imagination that any additional person who knew about it could cause a leak.

Finally Noah took me aside and said quietly, "It's on your property so it's your decision."

"We need to know how to read the carvings."

"You know we're going to go through the portal whether we can read where we're going or not and whether it's safe or unsafe."

We were silent for a moment. I finally said, "I want to at least have a reasonable expectation of returning safely."

"So we're going to show him the rock formation?"

"We are."

While we talked Ralph Williams had produced a pitcher of iced tea and what looked like a cake from a store. Instead of asking us immediately what we'd decided, he led the way through the kitchen to a tiny back yard and a picnic table that had seen better days.

"Have some tea and cake. Think over what you wish to do. Take your time. Know that whatever you decide I'll not say anything about the carvings to anyone. It would be unethical. But I suspect you'll never decipher them without help so if it's truly important to be able to read them then I'm your best bet."

He leaned back in one of the several old but comfortable chairs around the table and waited silently for us to make a decision. But we already knew what we were going to do. "When is a good day for you?"

A smile split his elderly face. He'd known all along what we'd decide. He'd most likely been through this exact same experience many times in the past when someone brought him something only he could decode that they wanted kept secret. "Is tomorrow too soon? Because I am quite eager to solve this unique puzzle."

CHAPTER 10

We reached the rock formation the following afternoon. Noah picked me up fairly early and we drove to Whitehall to get Ralph Williams – who asked us to call him Ralph – after which we headed to Noah's ranch and went the rest of the way on horseback with the stones safely in a cloth bag hanging from my saddle. Even with an early start it was afternoon by the time we reached our destination.

When the rock formation came into view, I glanced at Ralph to judge his reaction to the out-of-place structure. It was what I expected. "Unusual. Unlike others in the area." His attention ticked up with the object of his interest in sight though his voice was carefully neutral.

When the horses were comfortable with water, grain, and enough room to move, he walked as close to the rock carvings as he could get with the fake greenery in the way. He considered it and turned to us. "You hid the carvings behind artificial brush. You don't want it to be found." Still said in a neutral voice.

"How'd you know it was fake?"

"Because there's no greenery in the pictures you showed me. It didn't grow overnight so it must be artificial and the fact that it looks real means it wasn't cheap." His eyes narrowed. "You are serious about keeping this place a secret." His face said he wondered why we'd gone to so much trouble.

Our answer was to remove the fake greenery and he stepped close and leaned in to see how the carvings were made. He traced a couple lightly with one finger. Then he stepped back to get a decent view of the entire carved area.

But he said nothing. Since I was close enough to see his expression I saw why. He'd dropped so deeply into cryptographer mode that he didn't know we existed. Being that close I could also hear his musings. "Unique." "Never saw symbols like these before." "Must be old." "Ancient." "Older than the pyramids by thousands of years."

He finally snapped back to the real world. His brows knit. "I believe my first thought was right. These aren't letters that form words and this isn't a story and I believe most of the symbols are numbers. It's a catalog or something similar."

He pointed to the carvings. "Stories are linear in nature and these carvings aren't. Neither vertical nor horizontal and they are neither left to right or right to left. Each exists in its own square and is separate and apart from the others."

He examined them further. "I suspect the whole thing is a key of some kind with the individual symbols making many possible combinations because they seem to be in the kind of order you'd find on a combination lock with each symbol as easily accessed as every other one. In a combination lock there's a given sequence of numbers that will unlock it but the numbers are arranged in such a way that only people who know the combination can work it properly."

He saw the look that shot between Noah and me. "I'm right, aren't I? It's a key of some type and you knew that when you asked me to come here." We said nothing. "So why'd you bring me all the way out here in the wilderness and ask me to decode something if you already know how it works?"

He waited for our answer, knowing there'd be one. We'd brought him at considerable effort because we needed his expertise. Noah gave me the same look as when it had to be my decision to bring Ralph here because the rock formation was on my property.

Now, too, it was my decision and for the same reason. So I gave Noah the same look and slight nod that I'd given him then and he spoke for both of us. "We will answer your question by showing you something."

"I presume it has to do with the carvings?"

"It has everything to do with them and when you see it you'll understand, though you are right that we do know what the carvings are for. You're here because we only know their purpose in a general way and we want to know specifically how they function. We *need* to know."

"You *need* to know?" Ralph repeated Noah's emphasis on the word 'need' and waited for further clarification with no emotion whatsoever. "Why?"

"Because it could be a matter of life or death."

Ralph was silent, waiting for a punch line that never came. "Okay, then. Show me what you have. If it appears you are right about its importance and if there's nothing illegal about what you're doing then I'll do my best to help. But I must repeat that these carvings don't resemble anything I've ever seen before or ever heard of so I'm not sure how much help I will be."

He moved slightly, irresolutely. "I'm a cryptographer. I'm not good with life or death." He folded his arms and stared at us. "So before we go further, perhaps I should make one thing clear. If anything I've said or done so far doesn't sit right with you, then I'll return to Whitehall before seeing what you plan to show me and I promise that I'll never divulge anything I do know."

Our answer was to lead him to the portal where we pulled aside the brush and pointed to the door-shaped indentation in the rock face.

His disappointment was obvious. "It's just an indentation in the rock that resembles a doorway. The indentation and the carvings are probably not related."

"They are related and it's more than an indentation. It's an actual doorway."

"So you want me to decode the carvings because you believe my doing so will enable you to open a rock that you hope is a door to another world?" He clearly considered this to be a wild goose chase.

"It is a door. A portal. We know so because we've already opened it and visited two of the worlds on the other side."

His sharp intake of breath was the only indication of how hard our words hit him but he still wasn't convinced of the truth. Noah spoke quietly. "We want to continue to travel through those worlds and we want to do so safely and in some kind of order. So we must understand the symbols on the carvings. We must be able to read the map of those worlds. As I said before, it's a matter of safety."

I took over the explanation. "We have so many unanswered questions. Are those worlds dangerous? How many worlds are there? Will the portal change while we're in another world and prevent our return?"

Another quick intake of breath said he'd heard but still didn't believe us as he said simply, "Prove it."

We pointed to the portal. He approached it tentatively. Touched it. Jumped when his hand went through. Took several steps back and turned to us in a kind of shock. "You're telling the truth. It is a portal."

"And we need your help to decipher the carvings and decode the mechanism that makes the portal work.

The combination lock. Because we plan to keep visiting other worlds until we find the key that'll lead to a million strange and wonderful places that we can visit at will."

He went silent for several long minutes during which we waited for him to internalize what had just happened. The concept was as mind-boggling for him as it had been for us. Then he spoke. "You say there are numerous worlds?" We nodded. "And you believe the carvings dictate which world the portal opens onto?" We nodded again. "What makes you think that?"

"Because it has changed worlds. Twice so far. We're fortunate we were on this side of the portal when it happened."

Another long silence. "I'll do my best but it'll be a challenge because there's not much to go on." Noah and I looked at each other and again he caught the look. "There's more, isn't there? Something you haven't told me. I see it in your faces. What do you know that I don't know that I must know if I'm to help?"

I went to my saddle and brought back the bag of stones. "We found these in the first world we visited. We didn't know what they were for until I accidentally touched one to the rock carvings and the next time we opened the portal we found it had opened onto a different world."

I gave him the stones. As he pulled out one from the bag I said, "They look alike. I don't know which one it was that touched the rock formation."

He compared them. "They are most likely identical copies of a master key and they exist for the same reason locks come with at least two keys. Redundancy."

He held them up to examine them in the afternoon sun. We watched as one expression followed another across his face. Then he returned the stones to the bag. "I believe I have enough information to begin."

The man was amazing. A true scientist. He walked over to the carvings and examined them as if they were merely a foreign language that he'd decipher in due time because it was what he did. Judging by how quickly and smoothly he'd assimilated what had taken us days to learn and accept and considering he'd done so without turning a hair or showing any outward sign of shock we knew he was the right man for the job.

"It would help if I could see for myself how the portal operates and you could show me some of those different worlds. I want to observe the carvings as the portal opens. See if anything happens when it changes."

He was in full professor mode. "I don't need to enter the world itself but it will help me figure out how it works if after visiting it you describe each world to me. Perhaps similar combinations lead to similar worlds."

We checked out ten different worlds over the course of the next few days, going home every night and returning after picking up Ralph in town. Ten! We never found the original world, the one with the safe, nor did we again encounter the world of snow and ice.

But there was enough variation among the worlds we did find for him to make a leap of understanding judging by the gleam in his eyes that grew brighter with each new world.

One world was desert, with shifting sands and a double sun. We thought we heard something move on the other side of a sand dune but we didn't stay long enough to find out, nor did we climb it to see for ourselves because that would mean straying farther from the portal than we were comfortable doing.

Another was jungle complete with strange birds that sang raucously and undergrowth that was every color in the spectrum. It was awesomely gorgeous and I couldn't wait to leave because the vines and other plant life grew so close together and were so tightly intertwined that we couldn't possibly enter the jungle itself and it was so thick that any deadly life form would be hidden from view until it was too late.

Another was barren. Nothing living that we could see, merely rocks and cliffs and mountains continuing into the distance with a blustery wind blowing sand and dust into tornado shaped vortices that swirled and danced in a kind of unseen rhythm that bent and swayed and cried out with a kind of otherworldly music. But we could breathe and we weren't sure how that could be without plants and photosynthesis. We asked Ralph about it when we returned home and he looked it up online.

"Ultraviolet light can do the same. Breathable air

created without plants."

"Is it dangerous for humans?"

He didn't know but I watched myself for signs of illness for the rest of that day and the next until I was reasonably sure neither Noah or I had been somehow poisoned. But we were fine.

Every world was different from every other one and each trip was unique in some way but as the trips added up, we grew more and more comfortable visiting other worlds. Except that we had no control over where we went.

Every trip began with either Noah or I brushing a stone against the carvings. Ralph would watch as we touched the carvings and carefully mark where contact had been made on the picture he'd brought with him that was spread across his knees.

After many worlds, he said, in a slightly weary voice, "This is a rather large picture of the carvings. It was made from numerous smaller ones taped together. A table would be nice." As he spoke, he made still another mark on the portion of the picture on his knees. Then he rose slowly and with difficulty.

I was filled with guilt that I'd let this elderly man work in such an awkward position while all Noah and I did was to step through the portal, look around, and reappear with a description of the world we'd just visited. We were tourists, he was curled into an uncomfortable knot. "Enough for one day,"

Noah felt just as bad. "Tomorrow we'll bring

whatever you want to make your job easier." His shoulders moved, a sure sign of feelings of guilt. "But you don't have to come tomorrow if you don't want to. You need a break and there's no urgency."

Ralph did look truly tired but at Noah's words he straightened to his full five feet something. "Wild horses can't keep me away from this find." He shaded his eyes and inspected Noah and me. Up, down, and sidewise. "Do you realize what you have here? It's easily the most important find in human history and I intend to watch it unfold if it's the last thing I do."

"What *we* have here," Noah corrected him and I could have kissed him for including Ralph. "You're as much a part of whatever this is as Emma and I. Possibly more because you are the key to making the whole thing work."

"It's an awesome project," Ralph said somberly. "There is a key, I'm sure of it, and I promise to find it."

His comment about a key reminded me of something I hadn't been able to put out of my mind. I explained about finding the safe containing the stones in the first world we visited. "No other world so far has had a safe. So I'm thinking that world might contain the key to the mystery of the portal as well as a safe. If we can ever find it again."

Noah started replacing the fake bushes to hide the portal and the carvings because the day's work was done. We all helped and soon the area looked as if no one had been there for years. Noah stepped back and considered our work. "Tomorrow, this place will be different with a table and who knows what else we'll need to do the job right. No more hiding behind fake green stuff."

"It'll look like we're camping. That's a normal thing and shouldn't raise questions if anyone comes along."

Ralph pointed a short distance away. "There's a creek. A perfect place for a camping vacation during a lovely time of year."

Noah gave a deep belly laugh. "Not that we need to hide anything. If someone should see the portal, they'll think it's fake and we're making a movie."

We all laughed. It was a good release of the tension that had held us in thrall.

The next day started out like the previous one. Noah picked me up, we both picked up Ralph in town and then we all went to Noah's ranch and from there we rode horses to the rock formation. Except this time we brought a pack horse with a tent, lots of gear, and a couple folding tables and soon the space beside the creek could pass for a real camp site.

CHAPTER 11

"If it's okay with you two, I'll stay here tonight." Ralph looked over the campsite when the day's work was done. "It looks comfortable and my staying here will save time tomorrow. I'll be up and working when you two are just waking up."

So the next day we brought more equipment. A cot to save him from having to sleep on the ground, plus cooking equipment and food in coolers. Ralph spent much of his time at one of the tables from the first day, deciphering the carvings while the other became a de facto kitchen. His coffee was to die for.

We soon learned not to bother him because he was usually lost in decryption efforts but he did look up from his work now and then. One time his face was wreathed in smiles because he had good news. "I now know enough to prevent the portal from changing while you're in another world. I may not yet be able to read the symbols but I've figured how to lock the portal."

We were overjoyed. "We can stay longer and go

farther afield." Until then each time we'd stepped into another world, we'd merely looked around and stepped back out. "We can search for more safes and anything else that might tell us how the portal was created and by whom."

Noah, especially, celebrated the idea of longer stays. "We can use my walkie-talkies. They go thirty to forty miles. We'll be able to describe each world to Ralph as we explore it." He was eager to move beyond brief, cautious visits.

His whole body was a coiled spring every time we stepped through the portal. I suspected it was all he could do not to throw caution to the winds and go far beyond the portal even if meant he might never return. Possibly the only reason he hadn't done so was because he knew I'd object. Strenuously.

That night Ralph once again chose to stay at the camp. Noah and I returned to his ranch, promising to bring the walkie-talkies the next morning. When we got there we unsaddled the horses and he heaved the saddles over the side of an empty stall.

"It's nice that it'll be morning when we reach the rock formation instead of afternoon like it usually is." With the saddles taken care of we walked the horses. "Because we won't have to pick up Ralph from Whitehall. That'll save hours."

"I'll get going as soon as I wake up. If you have the horses ready we'll get a really early start."

Noah looked around thoughtfully. "Maybe there's

a better way." He slanted a look at me. "But it'll be your decision. Of course." He spoke so casually I knew he'd planned his next words and probably practiced the best tone of voice to use to talk me into whatever he was thinking about. "We'll save a lot of time if we can use your place as a base of operations."

The horses were cool so we put them in the barn as he explained the reason for my place instead of his. "Your cabin is closest to the rock formation and if we start from there we won't need horses. They are only necessary to get across the creek because there's no bridge and to get through an area of rough, rocky terrain that we can't avoid if we come from my place. Neither will be a problem if we come from a different direction."

With the horses secure for the night we crossed the yard towards my car as he explained more. "We'll have to use my truck, though. Your tiny car wouldn't last a minute off road but my truck can get there with no problem and has enough dents and dings that a few more won't be noticed."

His idea would save hours each day. "If we do what you're suggesting and all of us stay at my place then my generator can power Ralph's computer. He needs it for research and I noticed that he brought extra batteries."

The more I thought about Noah's idea, the more I liked it. "I can pick up more fuel for the generator next time I'm in town. Plus the cabin is large enough for all of us if we are willing to be a bit cramped." Except for one problem. "But what about your horses? You can't leave them alone."

"I can leave them with the Johnson family. They are the next ranch over on the opposite side from you. Nice people. Their kids love to ride and they only have one horse for four kids so I'm pretty sure they'll be thrilled and the horses can use the exercise."

"Tomorrow let's see how Ralph feels about the whole thing."

When we reached camp the next morning, Ralph informed us that he wanted to go home that night. "I need a shower and clean clothes and I'm not crazy about cooking over a camp stove." He was apologetic because he knew how much time that would add.

I told him what we were thinking of doing. He agreed immediately.

It took a couple days for everything to be moved from wherever it was to my cabin and during the move nothing got done at the rock formation but when we finally settled into my cabin the accommodations were comfortable and only slightly cramped. Ralph promised to make coffee if Noah and I would do the cooking.

The next morning, our first as a threesome, we had a hearty breakfast and brought enough sandwiches to last the whole day and two thermoses filled with coffee and we were at the rock formation shortly after dawn. Noah had brought the walkie-talkies. "Our substitute for cell phones."

"Wouldn't make any difference if we had cell phones because there aren't cell towers in the other worlds." Over twenty of which we'd visited thus far.

The walkie-talkies were wonderful. That fact was huge because when we stepped through the portal and found ourselves in strange worlds we now knew someone would be at the portal who could make sure it didn't change while we were gone and we could communicate with that person.

I'd never thought of myself as a coward and I'd never feared stepping into all those different worlds but I was kind of glad we'd never strayed far from the portal. Now that would change.

But I truly was eager to explore because each world was fascinating in its own way. I wanted to learn about as many worlds as possible. I wanted to find another safe or know for sure there was only one. I wanted to learn the secret of the portal. I wanted many things and now I could go after them.

But beneath my eagerness, each time I'd stepped through the portal there'd been a slight but very real thrumming in my belly beneath that eagerness and I was always glad to return to our home world. To Wyoming. To safety.

The walkie-talkies and Ralph's assurance that the portal wouldn't change while we were away diminished the thrumming and sent it to such a distant part of my brain that I was able to ignore and get on with the exploration of more worlds than I'd have thought existed before we found the portal.

That night, our second after moving into my cabin, after dinner and some of Ralph's amazing coffee, I got out blankets for him to sleep on the homemade couch Uncle Cantrell had made that had contained the stones in a hidden compartment. I had a portable bed on my shopping list but until then the couch was comfortable.

We already had the stones we'd found in a hidden compartment in the couch so I felt foolish looking for further hidden compartments as I spread out the blankets. But I did look. And I found a second board on the opposite end of the couch that was similar to the one that had covered the first compartment.

Another hiding space? Without mentioning my discovery to either of the men who were busy washing dishes I knelt down and pushed at the board. I gasped when it opened. Ralph didn't notice but Noah did and gave me a sharp, questioning look. When he saw what I was doing he put down his dish towel and joined me. "What did you find?"

I pulled out a book. It had no title but was thick. I opened it curiously. It was almost full of handwritten notes. "It's Uncle Cantrell's journal."

Ralph had joined us by then with a puzzled expression. "Isn't this where you found the stones?"

I nodded as I paged through the journal. It was written in a careful, precise script with each entry dated. It went back several years. "He wrote about his travels beyond this world."

Dishes were forgotten as we settled down to learn what my uncle had written. We followed his journeys through the worlds we'd already visited and many we'd not yet found. After getting Midnight he'd taken the dog with him on his journeys. For protection, he wrote. Midnight was large and tough and not afraid of anything and the two had made a good team.

In the journal he described finding Midnight as a puppy that had been abandoned by its mother in one of the many worlds he'd visited. He saved Midnight's life and the dog recognized that fact and was soon a good battle companion when things went south. He said Midnight had been a runt so we couldn't imagine how large normal sized dogs were in that world.

"We should take him with us after this." Noah spoke quietly, catching my attention over Ralph's shoulders.

"Not until we know how to communicate with him and know he'll protect us as he protected Uncle Cantrell." Noah's nod said he agreed and we silently made a pact to spend time with Uncle Cantrell's over-sized Labrador when we had time. Except we now knew he wasn't a Labrador after all. He merely resembled one.

The journal entry about Midnight reminded me of that first day when the dog had tried to go through solid rock while chasing a rabbit. Now I realized what had actually happened. He'd thought he could go through because he'd done so many times before.

We kept reading so we learned that Uncle Cantrell's favorite world was the one where he'd left the safe with the stones. He called it 'Seashore' and I could understand his preference for such a lovely, serene place.

Noah had other ideas. "I look forward to exploring it when we find it again because there might be more than just a lovely beach there." He didn't say he thought it was the key to the portal but I read the hope in his face.

Most important, though, was the casual mention of the stones in the journal. Seems Uncle Cantrell had gotten lost in one of the many worlds he visited. He thought he'd have to spend the rest of his life there. But as he unloaded his pack and spread everything on the ground to evaluate what he'd have to depend on, he noticed that as he dumped the stones out of their pouch, they all landed with the end with a hole in it pointing in the same direction.

'Those stones got me home. On a hunch, I took off in the direction the stones were pointing and eventually I found my way back to the portal. In addition to their other attributes, they function like a homing device.'

Noah closed the journal and looked at me. "That'll make exploring worlds much safer. Enough so that I vote to start actual exploration of at least some of the worlds we encounter. We know we're going to do so eventually. Why not now?" Neither Ralph nor I could argue with him because he was right.

Eventually Ralph put the journal on the table and said he was tired. Noah and I were too excited by the discovery of the journal to sleep but we didn't want to keep Ralph awake so we adjourned to the porch and settled down on the steps with hot cocoa and a million stars to wait for the strange energy that was keeping us awake to lessen enough that we, too, could sleep.

Noah pointed to the sky. "Most of them have planets. I wonder which ones we've visited." The night was warm and fuzzy and the clear night sky was a place of black velvet with millions of diamonds scattered across it.

"I wonder how many of those planets we will someday reach through the portal." Thinking about the possibilities made me hug myself. Misreading my action, Noah moved closer and put an arm around me, warming me, relaxing me. And causing a warmth to begin somewhere in me that had nothing to do with either the night or the temperature. A man-woman kind of warmth.

Unaware of his effect on me, he said, "All of them, perhaps."

I could have pushed Noah away or told him I wasn't cold but I did neither. Instead I moved ever so slightly closer. His response was to wrap his arm around me more securely. And so we sat and watched the stars and thought about the planets circling them that we might already have visited or would visit at some future time.

Which brought up a question. "Why has every world we've visited been one with an atmosphere and the right gravity? One where we could just step in and start living?" We were so close that Noah's words were whispered because there was no need to speak louder though we both pretended it was to avoid waking Ralph.

"Does the portal scan each world to make sure it's suitable for people?" I turned to see his reaction to my thought.

"Considering how many worlds we've visited so far and that we've never had a problem except the one world of ice and snow – and that could have been because it was winter -- we should make the assumption that is precisely what it does." His words floated through the warm night air and it didn't matter what he said or how he answered, I was happy with his deep baritone against the close rustling night sounds and an owl hooting somewhere far away.

"We should ask Ralph what he thinks." I spoke only after a long pause because it took a while to find my voice. I'd somehow lost it because of being close to Noah.

"I'm sure he'll agree. He's probably already taken it into consideration along with many more details we haven't yet thought of."

We sat thus for a long time. I had no idea how long because time lost its meaning in that dark, warm night. Something had been lurking inside of me from the first moment I saw Noah and had grown incrementally ever since. In that darkness the feeling came to fruition with a suddenness that made me breathless. Love? I didn't know but thought it might be.

I licked my lips and wished I didn't feel the way I felt because we had a thousand worlds to explore and no time to consider anything else. No time for a relationship beyond being partners in exploration. No time for romance. That would be true even if Noah felt the same way about me that I now felt about him. Which he didn't. Anyway, no matter how either of us felt, we had no time for the two of us because we had worlds to explore.

CHAPTER 12

The next day, when I brought up the subject, Ralph agreed that the portal did more than just provide an entry to other worlds. It also made sure those worlds were suitable for human habitation. "I noticed that aspect immediately. I expected you two to have to jump back without stepping completely through and I expected it to happen often because the world beyond would be uninhabitable. Deadly even. But that never happened. The only explanation is that the portal was programmed for people. Which means people made it."

He was thoughtful, even more so than usual and his usual demeanor was that of a college professor so deep in researching something or other that they didn't know the world existed. "But what people programmed it? Where were they from? And can we find them and their world?"

He sighed. "And why can't I decode their language? I so wish I could program the portal to visit a specific world. All I can do is lock it when it opens onto some world of its own choosing." He smoothed his shirt and squinted into the morning sun. "But I'm good at what I do. So that'll change."

"Uncle Cantrell's favorite world was the first one we visited. The one with the safe. That must mean something."

Noah had been listening. Now he spoke. "It could merely mean he liked white sand beaches and clear blue oceans."

Ralph looked from Noah to me and back. "There are a thousand possibilities. We'll learn them all. Eventually. If we get back to work."

So we went to the portal and resumed visiting whatever world it opened onto with Ralph trying all kinds of ways to control the process. But our seemingly pointless discussion had one positive result. Instead of just visiting the worlds, we started classifying them. Naming them. Describing them in a journal similar to Uncle Cantrell's only this one belonged to Ralph.

"Do all college professors carry journals wherever they go or is Ralph Williams unique?" Ralph was so deeply engrossed in his work he didn't know Noah and I were talking about him. "Not that journals are evil. But I don't have one in my back pocket and I don't believe you do either."

I picked up the journal belonging to Ralph that I'd been filling with a description of the world we'd just exited. Endless red rocks that made the water in lakes and rivers resemble blood and we saw nothing even close to trees at all. Just some kind of odd creeping stuff that reminded me of soot. "I can understand Uncle Cantrell preferring the first world. It was lovely." But I still believed there was more to that world than just sand beaches. It was a hunch but hunches are often right.

As for Noah, he left the journaling to me. Not his thing, he said. His love was the adventure of new worlds, all of them, and he had no favorites. He loved the differentness of them. The challenge inherent in the unknown. The sheer unexpectedness of each new place.

When I'd finished my journal entry we got back to work. We stepped into a world we named "Prairie" because that was what it was. A prairie.

Noah wanted in the worst way to explore it in more depth than a brief visit. "It's so much like Nebraska. Flat land with grass so tall we'd disappear in it if we walk anywhere. But we can get the horses and check it out that way." He finished with, "It's about time we check out some world with more than just a glance."

It was true that the vastness of the grasslands that opened before us as we stepped through the portal was awe inspiring and much like the American West. "The horses can run their hearts out in that world." He looked at me, the novice horsewoman. "You can do it, Emma. You can ride a galloping horse. I know you can."

He was hopeful more than sure of his statement but the prairie was inviting and Ralph agreed that we should start exploring in depth so we drove Noah's truck to his neighbor's place and borrowed his horses back for a day. We brought a large, rambunctious roan named Hazy for Noah and sweet, easy-to-control Cutie-Pie for me.

We rode them through the portal and learned what the old West must have been like. No fences, no telephone poles, no houses. Nothing but prairie and sky and wind and it was exhilarating and I managed not to fall off even though it felt like I was riding like the wind.

If course I was an inexperienced rider so it didn't take much to make me grab Cutie-Pie's mane for safety. The horses were probably cantering instead of galloping but I enjoyed the experience and began to understand Noah's love for exploration because putting distance between us and the portal was freeing.

And dangerous.

I never knew where they came from. It was as if they suddenly appeared all around us. Creatures with six legs and large, jagged teeth and fur so long it trailed the ground. They rose up out of that tall grass. They were so large their eyes were level with ours and we were on horseback.

They came towards us, running with an all-out rolling six-legged gait. Their mouths were open, their teeth pointed, and they howled with a high-pitched scream that penetrated my very being.

The horses panicked. They looked around wildly for a way to escape. And then they bolted through the only opening in the circle of strange creatures that would give them a chance to get through without being eaten. They ran all out.

The monsters followed but weren't built for speed and the swift horses outran them as I bent over Cutie-Pie's neck and grabbed her mane with all my might and managed to stay put. Beside me Noah, the expert horseman, had no problem. As we covered ground at a manic pace with Noah nearby trying to control Cutie Pie by herding her sidewise with Hazy so I'd not be tossed, the screams of the attacking monsters lessened and eventually died away.

When we were sure we weren't being pursued, we pulled the horses to a stop and got off. They were blowing and sweat foamed on their withers but they were no longer panicky. We walked them to quiet them down, aware that while we were on the ground the grass of this world was taller than we were so if more monsters lurked nearby, we'd not see them.

I moved closer to Noah. It seemed prudent to be near each other in case something else went wrong. Noah reached out and took my hand and we proceeded through the tall, waving grass as if walking through water. It was that thick.

As we walked, I told myself that the horses would sense danger. I hoped. Anyway, they needed a rest because if there were more monsters between us and the portal, they'd need to be fresh. They might need to run once more before we reached safety.

After a few minutes of uneasy walking, we remounted and walked them slowly and calmly until they seemed to have gotten past what had happened. Then we looked around for the portal but saw nothing.

We didn't know how far the horses had run in their panic escape but the landscape had changed somewhat. No longer completely flat, the terrain was now broken by occasional boulders here and there. We pulled up to the largest and checked it for vermin.

We were still spooked by the unexpected appearance of the monsters. They'd been the first animal life seen in any of the worlds so far, though we had heard noises in a few of them. Of course, this was the first world we'd explored beyond sight of the portal so it stood to reason we'd eventually run across native wildlife. I just hadn't expected it to have six legs and teeth that could rip me to shreds.

When we were reasonably sure there was no other deadly native life form on the boulder, we climbed it and surveyed the landscape from its slightly higher level but we still couldn't see the portal. "Good thing the stones are a homing beacon." Noah's voice was quiet and calm and I wondered how hard he worked to sound so reassuring.

He sounded as if being attacked by other-worldly monsters was hardly worth mentioning. It was an act. "We'll be home in no time." Then he dumped the stones on the boulder, and we watched as they moved until they all pointed in the same direction. Then we set off once more, each of us holding a stone to check direction every once in a while.

Once during the trip back, Cutie-Pie reared wildly, hooves flailing as I threw myself forward and grabbed her mane again, hanging on for dear life. When she came down, she danced and sidestepped something on the ground that moved sinuously and disappeared in the ever-present long grass before Noah could get a good look at it. I didn't even try.

What if I'd fallen off? What was that thing and was it deadly? I pushed the thought away because we had a long way to go and I needed to keep my mind on reaching safety.

We became ultra-alert for anything and everything. I wished the grass wasn't so high and didn't do such a good job of concealing whatever lived in this world that was so lovely until it tried to kill us.

Moving slowly and carefully we had no more incidents but it was hours before the portal came into view. We'd already contacted Ralph with the walkie-talkies and brought him up to date. He was concerned but there wasn't anything he could do to help beyond making sure the portal would bring us back to our own world once we reached it.

I breathed a sigh of relief when I saw the portal and urged Cutie-Pie forward, looking back to see if Noah was doing the same. So, I was sidewise when the monsters came at us and didn't see them. I wasn't prepared for them. I couldn't grab Cutie-Pie's mane.

Couldn't do anything.

I fell. I hit the ground hard enough that I blacked out momentarily. When I came to, I looked up to see Cutie Pie dancing skittishly in terror. I tried to get up but the world went haywire. And the monsters were between us and the portal.

Noah, the consummate horseman, saved my life. In less time than I'd have thought possible he was off Hazy and by my side. He pulled me up roughly with one hand as he grabbed Cutie Pie's reins with the other. "I'll help you on. Then ride her! You can do it! You must do it!" Without warning, he lifted me onto Cutie Pie even as he pulled her reins hard to bring her under control. She fought him but he was the horseman. The master.

Though she was still terrified she stopped fighting and let me get my feet in the stirrups. Then Noah shoved the reins at me while keeping an eye on the monsters. "Don't wait for me. Get through the portal." And he slapped Cutie Pie on the rump.

I thought the slap would frighten her even more and she'd bolt. But Noah had made sure she was facing the portal. She could see it and knew it meant safety so, even though reaching it meant going through the monsters, she ran full speed towards it in full panic mode as I held on for dear life.

The monsters clawed at us as she swept through them. I felt the wind of their reaching and Cutie Pie screamed as claws ripped at her body.

CHAPTER 13

We charged full speed through the portal. Cutie Pie was so terrified she didn't stop when we were in our own world. Instead, she kept running flat out, ears back from sheer terror, and all I could do to control her was to turn her so she ran in circles instead of heading for miles across the Wyoming landscape as I prayed the blackness that still threatened me would stay away.

But as Cutie Pie realized where she was and that she was safe she slowed and finally stopped at the little creek that meandered beside our campsite. And I slid off and looked for a place to sit before I blacked out. After a moment or so, I decided I was okay for the moment so I looked for Noah.

He was nowhere to be seen which meant he hadn't come through the portal. I panicked. I couldn't let him die in another world. So I took off running towards the portal. Noah was in danger. Or worse. So I ignored the blackness from my fall that threatened to overwhelm me as soon as I moved quickly. And I ran.

Before I reached the portal or the world turned completely black, Noah burst through on Hazy at a dead run similar to mine. But a monster was behind him climbing onto Hazy's back. As Hazy ran the monster reached for Noah. It was all he could do to control the frightened animal beneath him. He couldn't also fend off a monster three times his size.

The blackness came again, throwing me off balance. I couldn't do a thing except watch in horror as the monster crept along Hazy's back and closer to Noah.

But Ralph was prepared. Once we'd called him on the walkie-talkies and let him in on what was happening, he'd done more than just make sure the portal was open. He had a rifle in his hands, loaded and ready, and as soon as he saw the monster he raised it, aimed carefully so as to hit what he was aiming for and not Noah. And he shot the monster. It was a clean shot. It let out one last eerie scream, let go of Noah, and fell to the ground.

Noah let Hazy run off his terror much the same as Cutie Pie had done. He too, kept his horse going in a circle until Hazy slowed and stopped.

That was when I saw the claw marks on Noah's back where the monster had reached him and the much worse and deeper ones on Hazy. The horse's rump was a bloody mess where claws had ripped through his shiny roan coat.

I tried to run to Noah. I got halfway there before

crumpling to the ground with the blackness closing in on me but I saw Ralph ran to the monster and send two more bullets through its head. Then he came to see what could be done for two injured explorers.

He and Noah came to me first. "Go lie down." Ralph pointed to the tent. "Do you need help?" I didn't want to wimp out and I didn't think I needed help. I was wrong on both counts and Noah ended up holding me upright until he lay me gently on the cot we'd brought for Ralph and never removed.

Ralph joined us. As soon as he ascertained that I'd be okay once I had a good rest, he pulled Noah outside and tended to him and Hazy. His words were cryptic. "We clean the wounds and use as much antibiotics as we have available."

We'd brought a first aid kit but had expected to use it on scratches and scrapes from known threats. As I fought to stay awake in order to make sure Noah was okay, I hoped there'd be enough for both horse and man. My voice was groggy, but I managed to get my concern across. "Who knows what strange pathogens came through with that monster. We might not have any immunity against them."

Ralph had already stripped Noah's shirt off and was cleaning his wounds. He shook his head at my words. "I doubt that'll be a problem. The portal has existed for thousands of years and was created to travel between worlds so it only makes sense that pathogens traveled also. In time all joined worlds should have ended up with roughly the same pathogens so antibiotics that will help in one world will most likely help in all of them." Then he added in a whisper, "I hope."

Noah's wounds turned out to be surface cuts that took little time and minimal antibiotics to treat. When he was clean and had ointment on all his cuts Noah turned to Hazy. He led the horse into the creek where he washed his rump thoroughly. It turned out that his cuts also were superficial though deeper than Noah's.

"When we return the horses to the Johnson place, we'll tell them he ran through a patch of brush and that's where the cuts came from." Noah sighed. "And we'll not take horses through the portal again."

I thought back on what had happened and managed to speak clearly enough to be understood even though the blackness was coming closer with each passing minute. "Don't blame the horses. It was my fault. If I'd stayed on Cutie Pie, we'd have got through without a problem. As it was, I almost got you killed."

Noah saw it differently. At least he said so though in any case he'd have denied my guilt just because that's the kind of man he was. "It wasn't you. It was the horses. It happened because we brought them into a world they didn't know. They bolted when we first saw the monsters." I nodded because that was what had happened but it didn't lessen my guilt.

"We'd have been lost without the stones because the horses ran until they were too winded to go further and when they stopped, we had no idea where we were. That must never happen again and that means the horses stay here after this."

"Then how will we explore beyond the immediate area of the portal?" I blinked the blackness away a bit longer. "If we have to walk it'll take days to cross the ground we covered today."

Ralph had been listening. "I have a four-wheeler at my place in town."

"Won't work. Vehicles require fuel. How can we refuel in a world without gas stations?"

Ralph replied with the certainty of someone who'd done this before. "We use a trailer and I happen to have one. It's a big four-wheeler and a large enough trailer to carry both fuel and whatever else you need for safety and sustenance."

At that point the blackness took over and I fell asleep. Or lost consciousness. I never knew which it was, just that when I woke Noah was beside my cot. Ralph said he'd been there the entire time I was out.

I tried to rise but fell back before I managed to sit up. "Not yet," Noah said gently. "There's no hurry."

I never knew how much longer it was before I woke again. All I knew was that Noah was there as I knew he would be. This time he didn't let me try to rise by myself. Instead, he put an arm beneath my body and pulled me up so slowly that I didn't feel a thing. Then he sat beside me on the cot and kept that arm around me until I was sure I was okay.

Then he let go and I promptly threw up. I closed my eyes in embarrassment but all Noah did was get a pan of water and a washcloth and clean everything up, including me. Then he resumed his place beside me on the cot. We sat that way for a long time until I once more felt reasonably normal. This time I managed to rise and walk around without puking or falling over so we decided I'd live.

Then we went outside and continued the discussion of a four-wheeler and decided it would be a valuable addition to our expedition and we'd get it as soon as possible.

But before we could do that, the body of the monster needed to be dealt with. Midnight, who stayed with Ralph while Noah and I were in other worlds, seemed to be familiar with the monster. Because he'd been with Uncle Cantrell in the prairie world at some point? We didn't know but watched as the large, black Labrador circled the body with its hair up as low growls told us the monster was, indeed, extremely dangerous.

We finally decided on using the horses to haul the huge body back into the prairie world. We reasoned that if we buried it, animals could dig it up and it would then have to be explained. So we roped the horses to the body as if it was a cow.

They were skittish but Noah was an experienced horseman and they'd been trained to handle cattle so he finally got them to pull the body through the portal with Noah on Hazy and holding Cutie Pie so both could go through.

The body was a bit more difficult. I put my hand on it to make sure the horses could pull it through. I winced at the touch. The monster's coat was rough, like barbed wire, but it worked and soon the body was rotting in the sun of that other world while Noah and I and the two horses were back in Wyoming.

Then we waited for the claw marks on Hazy to heal enough to not be too noticeable. We didn't want any questions about them. So, it was a couple days before we returned the horses to the Johnson ranch so their kids could go riding. The kids were over-joyed, and I suspected both Hazy and Cutie Pie were happy to be with kids instead of monsters.

Several days after that, when Noah's wounds were reasonably healed and not noticeable, especially under a shirt, we headed for Whitehall to stock up on supplies and pick up Ralph's four-wheeler and its large, sturdy trailer.

When we left Whitehall, Noah's truck was groaning under the weight of all our supplies and was towing both the four-wheeler and its trailer. We resembled a parade, and we attracted attention. A couple of townspeople waved as we left, and Ralph guessed they'd tell everyone that Dr. Ralph Williams was on another one of his crazy expeditions. And they'd be right.

That evening at my cabin, after stowing supplies, we three were almost lethargic. Our reaction to what had happened was that pronounced. Only Midnight was full of his usual energy and ran from bush to cabin to shed and back. As usual. Ralph was inside making coffee but Noah and I watched the black Lab's antics.

"He's been to other worlds. We know that from your uncle's journal. He'll be helpful if we run into any more unfriendly natives." Noah sighed. "So, we'd best learn how to communicate with him. He must understand our commands and listen and obey."

Neither of us had tried to make Midnight do anything up to that point. We'd not had to either discipline or train him because he was a friendly dog that enjoyed being around us and when Ralph joined our family Midnight welcomed him without hesitation. But companionship was different than obeying commands.

CHAPTER 14

Noah had some hardtack. He threw a piece of it to Midnight to see what the dog would do. Midnight caught the hardtack in his mouth before it hit the ground. Then he brought it to Noah.

"Hey, boy." Noah rubbed Midnight's ears and the dog loved it. "You brought it back to me." Midnight looked Noah in the eye. "You could have eaten it instead. You know I'd not be angry because I can't be angry with you."

Midnight put his head in Noah's lap. "Are you asking permission to eat it?" Midnight stood alert in front of Noah, ears cocked, waiting. Noah handed him the hardtack and Midnight swallowed it in one gulp. "That was fast." The hardtack eaten, Midnight continued to stand before Noah with his tail wagging. Watching. Waiting.

Noah looked a question to me. "What does he want now?" I didn't have a clue but Noah decided more hardtack was a good guess so he threw a second piece.

Again, Midnight caught it in midair and brought it to Noah, then waited patiently but alertly until Noah handed it back to him. Then he again gulped his treat down." And put his head in Noah's lap.

"Looks like he's well trained." I joined Noah and Midnight. "Makes sense if Uncle Cantrell took him to other worlds. He'd not want a rogue dog loose in an unknown world." Midnight moved over to me as I spoke and stared at me much as he'd stared at Noah. "I wonder what commands he's used to."

We began Midnight's training the next day. We expected a long, difficult process. That didn't happen because Midnight taught us how to communicate with him instead of the other way around. "It's as if he's been waiting for this learning session ever since we came into his life. As if he knew all along that he was needed."

We regarded the huge, oversized black Labrador thoughtfully. Intelligence shone in those dark, doggie eyes. "Do you suppose he's been waiting all along for us to include him?"

"If so then he's a lot smarter than we've given him credit for."

"He's a Labrador Retriever. Labs are intelligent."

A bird spiraled down to perch on the porch railing. Midnight went after it with gusto but the bird flew away, leaving Midnight whimpering in frustration. Then Ralph came to the porch and informed us through the screen door that it was time to get dinner started and if we wanted it to be edible we'd better make it ourselves.

We scrambled because though Ralph's coffee was amazing, his cooking left a lot to be desired. The man was skinny for a reason.

Midnight proved to be amazingly patient with Noah and me. We'd start to teach him a command but often he'd give us a look that said the command was beneath him because he was a superior kind of dog. He'd then proceed to do whatever we'd been trying to teach him, and he'd repeat whatever it was over and over again until we'd realize he'd known all along what was wanted and how dumb did we think he was, anyway?

The only problem was that he didn't speak English. But he did know how to get his point across without words. Whenever we were particularly dense his tongue would hang out and he'd sit down and simply stare at us like a teacher might stare at a couple of unusually dense students.

"He was closer to Uncle Cantrell than I realized."

"He probably already knows more about the worlds beyond the portal than we do."

"And I now know what it feels like to be condescended to by a dog."

That evening Ralph informed us that he'd made somewhat of a breakthrough in deciphering the inscriptions on the rock face. "I'm just beginning to understand the intricacies of the portal but I'm getting a feel for how to use it even though I'm sure that knowledge is miniscule compared to the totality of the knowledge to be learned."

He explained that our visits no longer needed to be random. He could program the portal to return us to a specific world once we'd visited it. "I've been copying the symbols that lit up every time you two went through the portal. Different combinations open onto different worlds. I've marked the combinations for each world you visited. Except the first ones of course, the ones from before I was involved."

"So, there's no chance of finding the first world again?"

Ralph was silent for a moment. "I have an idea about that but it'll take some work to see if I'm right." He continued. "Many automatic gates keep a record of how they are used. I'd expect this one does too, at least to the extent of listing worlds in the order in which they were visited."

"So, the first world visited would be the first on the list?"

"By checking backwards, you should be able to find the original world?"

He nodded. "I believe so but I still can't read the list and even when I do figure that out I'll still have to figure the combination to enter that particular world."

"You'll do it." We knew Ralph. We'd accidentally stumbled on the perfect person for the job. It was merely a matter of time before we'd return to that first world.

Ralph went to bed and Noah, and I stayed up on the porch to watch the stars and discuss the next day's travels.

We agreed to take Midnight with us and discussed how best to utilize the four-wheeler. We decided Noah would drive the four-wheeler with me holding Midnight to monitor him until we got a feel for how he'd behave.

We trusted the dog after training sessions that had ended in learning he was already trained but we'd not been in a real-life situation with him so didn't know how things would play out when something unexpected happened.

We were eager to visit the next world and learn about it in depth with the additional resources of the dog and four-wheeler. We told each other that we were seasoned explorers and talked long into the night with the stars shining above and Midnight curled quietly at our feet.

We finally tiptoed inside so as not to wake a sleeping Ralph. As I headed for my bedroom, Noah stopped me. I couldn't see his expression in the dark but heard his breathing, deep and sure, as I waited for him to speak.

All that happened was a light touch on my arm before he turned towards his own improvised sleeping arrangement, an air mattress in a corner, and left me wondering what he'd wanted to say and hadn't.

I was antsy the next morning. Perhaps it was

because of the coming visit to still another world because this time we'd take our explorations to another level entirely. We were leaving our amateur status behind and becoming professionals as Ralph slowly, subtly, taught us how professionals went about their work.

The four-wheeler was the perfect vehicle. It was sturdy and top-of-the-line and had been used many times to get him to odd places to decode inscriptions on cave walls and ancient obelisks where he worked alongside archeologists. So, was that why I was nervous? Because of the expectation on me to be as good as those professionals? Or did I still wonder what Noah hadn't said in the dark of night?

Midnight was almost insane with excitement. When we started the four-wheeler and attached the trailer that was loaded with everything we might need, he knew what was happening.

He jumped in the trailer and refused to leave even though it meant we had to pack things around him. I wondered if Uncle Cantrell had had a similar vehicle and vowed to check out the shed behind the cabin carefully in case one was hidden in a corner. I suspected I'd find one.

But for now, we were well equipped for whatever the next world might be like. I climbed into Noah's truck, and we headed for the portal while Ralph followed in the four-wheeler. By the time he arrived, we were ready to go, and Midnight was running from the truck to the portal and back in his eagerness to get going.

We didn't know how we'd get the four-wheeler through the portal because a human had to touch everything that went through. I offered to ride in the trailer with Midnight in case that was necessary but we decided to first try with all three of us – Midnight, Noah, and me – in the four-wheeler to see if it would work. And it did. We passed through with no problems, trailer and all.

Then we stopped and looked around to see what kind of world we were in because, though Ralph could bring us back to a world we'd already visited, new worlds were still a roll of the dice.

The dice favored us this time. We found ourselves overlooking gentle hills covered with exotic plants and dotted with trees. Here and there forested areas bordered creeks we couldn't see but we heard the music of running water once Noah shut off the four-wheeler to better listen to this new world. Not to mention that he wanted to hear any potential danger. But there was none and so we relaxed as much as we relaxed in any alternate world.

"I think I'll like it here." Noah examined the blue sky and carpets of green all around us.

Midnight went insane with excitement. He jumped from the four-wheeler before I could grab him and ran in circles of joy. When he finally slowed, his eyes were happy, his ears were up, and his tail wagged happily.

"He's been here before," Noah stooped to pet the black dog.

"I wonder if Uncle Cantrell liked this world as much as Midnight does." I looked around and saw a small shed to one side of the portal. It was a clear sign someone had been here before. We approached it cautiously and laughed in relief when we got close enough to read the lettering on the boards that had been used to build it.

The unpainted wooden shed said Whitehall Lumber. "Uncle Cantrell came here often enough to justify building a shed."

There was no lock on the shed so all we had to do was unhook the latch and open the door to see what was inside. We found dog food. Before we could stop him Midnight was dragging one of the bags outside where he wrestled it open and dug into what he knew was rightfully his.

There was more than dog food. There were several cans of fuel. "So Uncle Cantrell did have a four-wheeler or something similar."

"Your uncle was an explorer of worlds. He had the proper equipment."

"I think this was one of his favorite worlds."

I remembered the monsters of the previous world and shivered. "I don't see danger here at all. Maybe it'll be paradise." We heaved one bag of dog food onto the trailer, called Midnight to jump in also, which he did gladly because he knew we were going exploring, and set off to see what this particular world was like. We were high on optimism and the knowledge that we'd be prepared for anything.

It was late in the afternoon and miles from the safety of the portal when we decided to spend the night there. We'd not encountered anything threatening and Ralph knew we'd thought about staying overnight and approved though we were at the farthest range of the walkie-talkies. They broke up several times during our talk but we got our message across.

Then we put them away and set up camp in a small clearing beside one of the many cold, rushing creeks with Midnight investigating each and every thing within a half mile of our encampment, tail wagging and ears up. It was clear that he knew this world, that he loved it and loved that he was finally a part of the team.

CHAPTER 15

The world had two moons. Each smaller than Earth's moon, they moved across the sky at different rates. We sat side by side before a campfire and watched the pattern made by their intricate dance cross the sky while Midnight, who'd settled down at last, curled nearby and watched the fire flicker in the light breeze that brought all kinds of exotic scents our way.

As I grew more and still more relaxed, Noah moved closer until our thighs were touching. I liked the feel of him close to me. His body was solid. Not that I was normally a fearful person but those monsters had done a number on my self-confidence and my lack of riding skills hadn't helped. Noah had saved my life and I recalled that fact as his arm went around my shoulders, and I sighed in contentment along with him. He poked a stick into the fire to make the flames flare and turned to Midnight to make sure he was far enough away to avoid being burned.

Midnight was no longer lying quietly. He was on

his feet, his head was up, his ears, though not laid back, were pricked in attention and his whole body was alert to something we could neither see nor hear. But we saw no fear or threat in his demeanor. Just awareness.

"What's out there, boy?" Noah spoke in a low voice. Midnight's tail wagged that he heard but he didn't move, didn't look our way. His attention was fixed on something beyond the firelight. "What do you know that we don't?"

Midnight looked our way briefly, then returned his attention to whatever we couldn't see. Then he whined. Not an angry growl. Not a fearful whimper. We couldn't imagine what was out there that brought such an unexpected reaction.

Noah's arm left my shoulder. He grabbed the rifle that he'd made sure was within reach. He aimed it in the general direction of Midnight's attention and thumbed off the safety. "Get the keys to the four-wheeler and be ready to get us out of here fast if anything happens." His voice echoed Midnight's demeanor. Not fearful but on high alert.

Something moved in the dark. Something so dark that movement was the only indication it existed. There was no form or shape to it. Just movement. Then it came closer and stepped into the firelight, facing Midnight.

It was a dog. A huge, black dog that could have been Midnight's twin except for size. It easily was double Midnight's weight and height, and Midnight was huge for his breed. But Midnight didn't back down. Instead, he made sure the newcomer understood this encampment belonged to us and that the larger dog was the intruder.

The newcomer came close. The two dogs circled each other as Noah prepared to shoot at the first sign of danger, following the movement of the intruder with the rifle. But neither dog started a fight.

Instead, they continued circling each other as they took each other's measure. Neither caved. We waited with held breaths for the outcome of this show of bravado.

The circling stopped. The two dogs touched noses as they took each other's measure. Then, as something unknown to us was decided, they became friends. Their tails started wagging and they sniffed each other head to toe.

Then the rest of the pack we'd not known existed until then came into the firelight. Four additional huge, black dogs. They could have been Labrador Retrievers except for their size. Each was bigger than Midnight. Much bigger. But otherwise, they were identical to him.

"I think Midnight is from this world," Noah said quietly, thumbing the safety back on and laying the rifle down, though closer to his body than before. Just in case. We sat without moving, without talking further, just watching as the pack and Midnight got acquainted.

"By his looks Midnight could be part of this pack. But by his size he'd be the runt of the litter. They definitely recognize him as one of their kind."

We watched for the better part of an hour, after which the pack left as silently as they'd come. We suspected they didn't go far because we didn't hear movement after they disappeared into the night and Midnight kept his attention where they'd gone. But he stayed with us, dropping back to the ground and putting his head once more on his paws.

We didn't sleep in the tent that night. We were too close to the forest to feel safe. Instead, we placed the sleeping bags on the ground between the fire and the four wheeler. Midnight stayed in his place, watching the part of the forest where the pack had disappeared until he, too, slept.

We slept fitfully. We took turns keeping watch. A precaution, Noah said, as he took the first watch. When it was my turn, I found myself watching Midnight more than the forest. He'd alerted us to the pack before, his behavior could alert me to danger now.

The sun of this other world wasn't up yet but the night was growing lighter, and the sounds of unseen animals changed as happens everywhere as night denizens go to sleep and those of the day awaken. I thought about waking Noah because it was almost his turn to take watch again but decided against it, choosing instead to watch a sunrise in what was a gorgeous world, albeit a potentially dangerous one.

So, I saw when Midnight awoke suddenly from slumber. This time the hair on his back was up, his ears were flat against his head and his body was tense. He growled. It was a low growl but the sound was unmistakable. Something was wrong.

I shook Noah and he came awake instantly. Sat up. Grabbed the rifle without me saying a word because he, too, saw Midnight. We slid out of our sleeping bags. I judged the distance to the four-wheeler and strained to see in the faint morning light that the keys were in the ignition. And we waited to see if this would be another false alarm or something else.

The sound, when it came, came fast and loud. Barking, howling and the sound of animals screaming in anger and pain. Many animals, too many to count by sound alone.

Midnight watched but made no move to go towards the sound and no animal of any kind came into our camp. But he kept guard, flicking glances from the forest to us and back again. Ready at any moment to do whatever needed doing. Totally on alert.

We moved to the four-wheeler and climbed on board. Noah's hand hovered over the ignition. But still we waited. Nothing had come into our camp, and we had no idea whether anything would.

Noah called Midnight, trying to get him to join us, but the big black Lab refused to move.

I also called with no success. "I wish he'd come."

"He's between us and whatever is happening out there. He's guarding us."

The cacophony grew louder. "Its's coming closer."

I couldn't take it any longer. I ran to Midnight and grabbed his collar. "You're coming now whether you want to or not." The large dog came reluctantly, still looking towards the source of what was clearly a fight.

Then the fight burst into the clearing. The tent was toppled in seconds as snarling, biting, fighting dogs overran it. "Shoot them." I screamed but the fighting packs didn't notice.

"Not Midnight's friends. I can't shoot them and every dog here is all black. I can't tell the difference." Noah's rifle was ready but he held off shooting.

One of the monstrous dogs turned our way, the largest by far of any in the fight. Saw Midnight beside us in the four-wheeler. Started for him, teeth bared, blood dripping everywhere, hatred in his every pore. Noah shot and the dog dropped.

The sound echoed through the clearing, a sound probably never heard before in this place. The fighting stopped as every wild dog looked for the source of the unknown sound. Midnight, being a hunting dog, wasn't bothered but he was the only dog that wasn't spooked. We waited to see what would happen next.

The attacking pack saw their leader down and investigated. They howled. We hoped they'd leave now they were leaderless. No such luck. After milling about for a few moments, they turned back towards Midnight's friends.

Noah shot again, over their heads this time and the sound stopped the imminent attack. Both packs turned towards the sound. Towards us. They didn't know what to do for moments. Then another dog in the attacking pack assumed leadership and started towards Midnight's friends.

Noah took aim and shot a second time a mini-second before the new leader reached out to take a bite out of one of Midnight's friends and that dog also dropped. Again, action stopped. For a moment.

Noah then resumed shooting, this time over their heads and the sound coupled with the deaths of two leader type dogs in a few moments demoralized the attackers and they left as quickly as they'd come, disappearing into foliage so thick we couldn't make them out even though the sun had now risen enough for it to be full daylight.

Midnight whimpered. He looked at his new friends. Two were dead. Another was bleeding badly and unable to stand. The others were in various stages of injury but walking and presumably would recover.

"Can we help?" Noah and Midnight both ran to the injured dog. It bared its teeth when Noah came near but didn't mind Midnight being nearby. "We have antibiotics." He left the dog and got the first aid kit from the four-wheeler. "If it'll let us near enough to do anything."

I didn't think it would. It was a wild animal, and we were an unknown element. But it had made friends with Midnight and all the dogs watched as Midnight stuck close to us. I petted Midnight, hoping the gesture would show them that Midnight wasn't afraid of us so maybe they shouldn't be either.

We approached the injured dog with the first aid kit. The live remnant of the pack came close and formed a circle around us. One false move by either of us and we knew we'd be torn to bits. But we wanted to make friends with this pack if it was at all possible.

Midnight had clearly come from this world, and he was a invaluable ally. More importantly, he'd become as emotionally attached to us as any domestic dog from Earth. So, the potential for friendship with the other dogs existed and we wanted to see if we could start a spark of something in this pack of wild animals.

We washed the injuries by dumping buckets of water from the stream over them and the dogs let us get the water and clean their pack mate, though their teeth were bared the whole time. But Midnight was with us so they just watched. And they watched some more as I carefully and very, very slowly applied antiseptic to the wounds. "It'll probably lick it off as soon as possible but at least we tried."

Then we backed away from the inured dog and the rest of the pack. We carefully and very, very slowly packed up the tent and dumped it into the trailer. Then we called Midnight. This time he was happy to join us on the four-wheeler. But we did one more thing before leaving. We dumped a pile of dog food from Uncle Cantrell's shed that we'd brought with us on the ground for the pack. As we left, they were already eating it. So, they knew what it was.

They didn't like the roar of the four-wheeler but when they saw that Midnight was on this unfamiliar thing and unafraid, they quieted and just watched as we left the clearing and headed for the portal. I was happy to go. I'd had enough of this world, at least for the time being.

But we would return. It was Midnight's home world and had been special enough for Uncle Cantrell to build a storage shed.

Had he been in the process of making friends with the native species? If Midnight could become his friend perhaps other dogs could also. Maybe we could finish the job he started and make friends with an entire pack. Some day. For now, though, we were headed home.

CHAPTER 16

I hoped for an uneventful trip home. It was a beautiful world, the weather was perfect, the sky a limpid blue and the packs of dangerous fighting dogs were behind us. But I took my cue from Noah's perpetual awareness and forced myself to be alert for whatever might happen. Like more wild dogs that didn't want interlopers in their world.

I did see packs in the distance but the unfamiliar sound of the four-wheeler kept them at bay. Then I saw a lone dog, a mother with puppies, lying in a spot of sunshine as her pups nursed. One puppy had become separated from the others and lay several yards away. It looked thin and afraid.

I pointed. "That puppy needs its mother."

Noah stopped immediately. If I wasn't already in love with Noah, then I maybe fell in love with him at that moment because who wouldn't love someone who'd stop to help a puppy whose momma would happily tear you to bits if you got too close?

Whatever the reason, something warm washed over me as he slowed and stopped. The pup looked our way. It was so sad and hungry and helpless I almost cried.

I had to help. I climbed down and approached slowly, cautiously, ready to run as fast as possible at the first sign of danger. When I was close, I saw that it was skin and bones. It wouldn't live much longer without its mother's milk.

I touched the tiny puppy, noticing how much smaller it was than the other puppies. It looked at me with hope. I tried pushing it closer to the mother, hoping it would be able to move on its own once I got it started so I could avoid what could be a deadly encounter with the mother.

The mother didn't seem to mind that I was there. She merely watched as I tried to get her baby close enough to nurse. But the other puppies did react. All of them. Instantly.

They scrambled toward me and the puppy and they were all snarls and bared teeth. They were puppies so their behavior was more for show than actually being dangerous, but they were large enough to do real damage and they made it clear they weren't happy with my presence. Or with my helping the puppy that was too far away to nurse.

They got close to the puppy and stopped. I backed a bit to see what they'd do. They ignored me and snarled at it. Pushed it over. Started to bite it. And the mother dog just watched. She didn't care.

I was horrified. The puppies were attacking one of their own. Fury at their behavior welled up in me. I yelled. Screamed.

That was when I noticed the dog pack beyond the mother. Black, like all packs in this world seemed to be. They looked my way. Some rose. Others bared their teeth. And they started towards me.

But when they reached the mother, she growled. She thought they were approaching her and she didn't want any of them near her puppies. So, they stopped momentarily, undecided what to do. How to handle this new threat. Me.

My screaming had worked. The puppies stopped harassing their litter mate and looked at me in confusion. They backed off slightly but continued to growl and show their teeth. They were a smaller version of the pack.

It was clear now how the lone puppy had gotten separated from its mother. Its littermates had frightened it away and the adult dogs were fine with that.

The puppy still looked at me. Hope shone in its eyes. Would I do something? Would I help it live? I answered that look and, ignoring the others and hoping they wouldn't do anything, scooped the puppy into my arms and ran as fast as possible back to the four-wheeler.

Noah was waiting, rifle at his shoulder and aimed at the pack beyond the mother. He examined the puppy in my arms. "It's half the size of the others. It's the runt of the litter."

"Like Midnight." We looked at each other as understanding dawned. "In this world, runts are pushed away and left to die."

He lowered his rifle because the pack hadn't approached further. "So that's how Cantrell got Midnight. The same way we are about to become the foster parents of a second black Lab." He put the rifle away, gunned the four-wheeler, and we took off. "If it lives long enough to reach our world and if we can find some milk and if we can figure out how to feed it then we've got a second guard dog when it grows up." Because if Midnight was any indication of what dogs in the world were capable of, then this pup would be amazing.

Noah glanced at it again as he pushed the four-wheeler to greater speed as the dog pack milled about and finally retreated. "It'll be as big as Midnight and that's huge in our world. But here, this pup is the size of a peanut."

When we returned to our world, Ralph's eyebrows rose at sight of the puppy. "And here I thought this was an exploratory expedition. Guess I missed something." He frowned as he saw how thin the poor thing was. He stroked it gently and it raised its eyes to him. "But puppies are cute."

He found powdered milk somewhere in the supplies we kept at the site. He mixed it with creek water that he heated on his tiny propane burner and then poked holes in a glove and offered it to the puppy.

The puppy guzzled it down greedily. Ralph examined the pup as it slurped up its first meal in a long time. "Kind of oversized, don't you think?" Then he added, "It'll be as big as Midnight."

"Even so, it's a peanut compared to its litter mates."

"Really?" Ralph considered the puppy again and almost as an afterthought said, "Peanut is a good name." The way he looked at that puppy told me that the two would become a team. A family just as if the pup had been born in our world. They looked right together.

Ralph guarded the portal and continued to work on decoding symbols while Noah and I took Peanut to the vet in Whitehall and got suitable puppy formula and also puppy food for when it could eat solid food. The vet eyed the small-large pup. "Part black Lab, that's easy to see. From the size of this guy, though, I think he's also part horse." We pretended not to have any idea about Peanut's parentage. He'd not believe us anyway.

He gave Peanut all the usual shots and declared him to be as healthy as possible considering he was near death from starvation but he thought we'd got him in time and that he'd live a long and healthy life. "He'll eat you out of house and home," was his parting comment as we brought Peanut out into the sunny streets of Whitehall.

After Noah carefully placed the puppy on a soft bed in his pickup truck seat so he could sleep we took advantage of our unplanned trip to Whitehall to stock up so we'd not have to return for a long time.

As we filled carts and loaded everything into the back of Noah's truck, I thought back to my spontaneous thought about being in love with Noah. I decided it hadn't been just a passing thought brought on by his humanitarian goodness.

In fact, there was no 'maybe' about it, something I realized with a kind of wonder because it was so unexpected. I was actually in love and as we perused groceries and decided which had a long shelf life, I looked back and tried to decide when it had happened. The actual moment.

It must have been coming for a while and I'd not noticed because exploring new worlds had a way of pushing other things out of one's mind. Now, thinking back, though, I remembered how, the day we met I'd been blown sidewise by his all-encompassing awareness of his surroundings and by the way he filled out a pair of jeans and a well-worn shirt.

But maybe that had been mere infatuation. Perhaps I truly fell in love when he saved my life from a bunch of monsters. It had been a life-altering situation so it might have happened then.

Or was it both of those times and more? Was it just being near him day and night while exploring new worlds? I plopped six cans of beans into our cart and wished I knew. But I didn't. I just knew how I felt.

Too bad he'd not shown any interest in me at all. None. Nada. As I added bags of rice to our supplies, I decided the bad thing about being in love was that we were so inextricably linked by the discovery of the portal that there was no way we'd part company, ever, and I'd have to live with a togetherness in which I felt one way and he didn't reciprocate.

Which meant there'd be no happily-ever-after for me. In fact, my future looked rather bleak. More like misery-ever-after. I told myself to suck it up as I dumped a half dozen jars of peanut butter into the cart and told myself I'd just have to live with the reality of being in love with someone who didn't love me back.

I also told myself in a very stern but silent voice that I'd figure out how to do that because I was determined to go as often as possible beyond the portal and I wanted to find its origin or know finding it was impossible. And both wants would involve being with Noah.

I couldn't imagine Noah not being a part of the endeavor any more than I could imagine myself falling out of love with him. But I could hope, I told myself, as we rolled our carts to the cashier. If it was possible to fall out of love with him, I'd do it. Somehow.

We returned to my cabin where, in a casual voice that amazed me considering I'd just made the mind-blowing discovery of unrequited love, I told Noah my thoughts about Uncle Cantrell perhaps having a four-wheeler somewhere on the property. He agreed that it sounded likely so we searched for it. Together. Side by side. Without the slightest hint of a romantic moment and now I wished for even a pittance of romance though a day earlier I'd not have given such an idea a second's attention.

We found both a four-wheeler and a trailer in a corner of the shed. It was under a canvas tarp with hay bales piled on top. Uncle Cantrell hadn't wanted anyone to find it. Which meant he hadn't wanted to explain why he had it. Which meant he'd used it for travels through the portal. We'd do the same.

We returned to the portal with Noah driving the truck with Peanut sleeping on a bed on the seat beside him and me driving the four-wheeler and pulling the trailer we'd found with it. The next time we entered a new world we'd be prepared for just about anything. Judging by what had happened in the last couple worlds we'd visited, two four-wheelers and a ton of supplies was the minimum necessary for such trips.

When we reached the portal Ralph was waiting with good news. "I found the first world you visited. The one you said has an ocean with a white sand beach and the safe that contained the stones." He examined the second four-wheeler with approval. "A real expedition can be mounted now. We can stay a long time."

"We?" Noah paused in moving Peanut's bed to a

comfortable spot in the sun while I followed with the small-huge pup.

"This time I'm going with you guys." Ralph folded his arms and stared Noah down, something I'd not have thought possible. "I figured out how the portal works. I found the world you think is of special importance. And I'm the only one here with any chance of decoding whatever might be found if that world turns out to be the key to the entire portal phenomenon."

Noah gulped. "That's all true." He turned to me. "What do you think, Emma?"

I nodded that of course Ralph would be included. "Because we can lock the portal, so we'll be sure to return to this world."

Ralph reiterated that we could do exactly that but said he was glad we still had the fake bushes to hide the rock carvings. "Not that it would make any difference if someone did find them. Once the portal is locked, they'd not be able to activate anything. But it's best if no one notices anything more than a campsite by a creek."

Noah checked the fake greenery. "We can position some of it so when we go through it'll fall into place behind us and hide the portal as well as the rock carvings."

Ralph was elated. I'd not seen him so excited since meeting him. "So as soon as we make a plan, we can leave."

I'd been listening. Now I spoke. "We get a good

night's sleep tonight and leave in the morning. No sense starting out tired." I looked at the two dogs, denizens of the last world we'd visited. "And we take both Midnight and Peanut because we can't leave either of them alone."

So, it was decided and we adjourned to my cabin to plan and stock two trailers with supplies for an extended visit. We included enough fuel for a long journey and would leave extra just inside the portal beside the safe that had once held the stones.

We made sure we had the stones with us. We divided them into two batches and put one batch in each four-wheeler. They'd become homing beacons if we got lost. Then we stocked lots of dog food for Midnight and puppy food for Peanuts.

We made a comfortable bed for the puppy in one of the trailers and decided Midnight would ride shotgun on the four-wheeler driven by Noah that would take the lead while Ralph would ride beside me carrying a high-powered rifle he said he could shoot with a fair degree of accuracy in the second four-wheeler that I'd drive with Peanut on a bed in the trailer.

We were ready.

Noah and I had been to many worlds by then. We considered ourselves experienced travelers. Still, the coming expedition felt different. Exciting. And scary. We'd possibly be gone for a long time and would go farther into an unknown world than ever before.

Who knew what we'd find? In spite of my

insistence that we get a good night's sleep I doubt any of us slept a wink that night. I know I didn't.

CHAPTER 17

We were unusually quiet when we passed through the portal. Once through, we stopped long enough to make sure the fake bushes had fallen as we wanted. Then we gave each other looks and climbed back onto the four-wheelers and set off towards the white sand beach that ringed a warm, blue ocean because we'd decided to follow the shoreline and only deviate from it if something grabbed our attention. No possibility of getting lost.

We stopped for lunch on that white beach that went for more miles than we could see. Even after hours of travel, the end wasn't in sight. After sandwiches, I dipped my toes in the water and wished I dared go swimming. It was that warm and inviting. I did convince Ralph and Noah to watch while I waded ankle deep but that was all I dared because we knew nothing about the sea so had no clue whether things in were deadly or not. Midnight, however, did go for a swim.

"He knows it's safe because he's been here

before."

"Or he's suicidal."

No sea creatures appeared. No monsters came at us from the thick undergrowth beside the beach. No packs of wild dogs attacked. The silence was eerie, broken only by the soft chirping of birds and the rustling of small animals in the forest.

"Nothing dangerous so far," Noah said unnecessarily that evening as we made camp on the beach instead of in the forest because from there we could see danger before it could reach us. But nothing happened that night. Or the next. The peace was almost surreal.

We could have traveled faster and thus gone farther. Instead, we meandered along the beach and watched for something – anything – that would catch our attention that could then become the focus of our exploration. None of us said so, but we all knew that by going slowly we'd be closer to the portal if things went south and able to retreat in short order.

But nothing happened and the weather stayed perfect with no change from hour to hour or day to day and the beach remained white and pristine. "This beach must go forever."

On the fourth day I grew bolder when we stopped to eat. I waded knee deep instead of just to my ankles as Midnight swam far out and returned to shake water all over us. Noah joined me in the water, hiking his jeans to his knees. Eventually, so did Ralph.

As we enjoyed ourselves, we kept watch for sea life that never appeared. And still, the only sounds were the wind soughing through the trees and the small animals and birds we heard but never saw.

"What kind of world has no , dangerous animals?" Ralph scowled as we began our fifth day of exploration. "And what's with the sameness of this world? The beach. The ocean. The forest. It's so perfect that it's almost as if someone designed it."

"Large animals might avoid the beach. Dangerous sea creatures might not come to the beach."

"They should exist. But we don't see any. Why not?"

"That's why the whole thing seems odd. Unnatural. Perfect."

"As in artificial."

"Exactly."

I thought aloud as I sought an explanation for the lack of large animals. "There must be animals and some of them must be large. There must be some because look at the plant life. Tall trees and all kinds of huge flowers. It's not a stubby, short world."

"This is a well-developed world that's way past the stage of life in which living things are tiny and can only swim and crawl and creep."

We'd learned a lot about evolution during our travels. Most worlds we visited were barren rock, but a few had plant and animal life and we'd quickly learned to gauge the stage of development by the size and variety of the plants and animals.

"This world is almost like Earth. Life has existed here for a long time. So, there must be more things running through the forest and swimming in the ocean than just the small things we hear."

It was an extremely beautiful world. And odd. So, the next morning Noah ventured into the forest to see what he could see. "I won't go far. I'll stay close enough to hear the waves so I can find my way back by the sound. But I want to find at least one of those things we keep hearing." He picked a spot where the vegetation was relatively thin and walked beneath trees as tall as the Sequoias on Earth. "Maybe they are larger than they sound."

I wanted to insist he stay where we knew it was safe because, now that I knew I loved him, I was selfish and wanted him to be safe. But of course, I said nothing. He'd think I was joking and would laugh. But I went close enough to the forest to keep him in view for a long time.

He was in the forest for almost an hour. When he returned, he was mystified. "No large animals that I could find. But the birds are a thousand amazing colors, and their songs are lovely." He shook off the detritus that he'd accumulated tramping through brush as he came close and took my hand. "Come see for yourself."

Ralph refused our offer to accompany us, saying he'd stay with the four-wheelers and watch over Peanut. As we entered the forest, he was relaxing on the edge of the trailer talking softly to the newest and smallest member of our team.

Noah was right about the birds. No tropical jungle on Earth had birds in such abundance and such variety. Red, blue, green and every other color imaginable and there were thousands of them, bursting out of trees as we approached only to return as soon as we were past. And they all sang.

"It's literally a paradise." I was transfixed by the colorful sight.

"Exactly." There was more Noah wanted to say but he held back.

Because he was afraid he'd sound foolish? "What is it? What are you thinking?"

"It's this whole thing – this whole world. I'm almost creeped out."

"Because it's beautiful?" He nodded and stopped, still holding my hand so I couldn't continue on as he forced me to think about what he'd said. "It's gorgeous and definitely odd. It's close to perfect and since perfection isn't possible the very beauty we are surrounded by makes me wonder how it came about. How it came to be. How it was created. And I think it was created. I believe someone or some thing made this world."

We walked a bit longer and then returned to the beach where Ralph and the dogs were enjoying the sunshine. We answered questions about the forest and the beautiful birds.

Ralph agreed with Noah. "It does sound odd though a perfect world is theoretically possible." Then he added another thought. "Or it's not what it appears to be." He thought some more. "An artificial world makes more sense than natural perfection."

"Who made it?" We looked around as if for ghosts but all we saw was sand and sea and sunshine after which we jointly decided we were being foolish and should enjoy the day instead of dreaming up reasons for it not to be real.

We camped that night, as usual, on the beach though we were beginning to think we didn't need to be quite as careful as we'd been so far. But we still kept watch with our agreed upon turns with one keeping watch while the others slept. My hours spent sitting on the four-wheeler with a rifle in hand were more to enjoy the three moons on the water and the sounds of night birds as I remembered how gracefully they'd flown overhead during the day than to watch for danger though I kept reminding myself that it could come unexpectedly. But it never did.

The next day we continued along the beach, looking for something different but not expecting to find it. Then, almost half-way through the day Noah slowed his four-wheeler and stopped. Following in the other vehicle, I looked around to see what had caught his attention. He was looking away from the ocean, towards the forest. I followed his look.

I saw hills except they weren't exactly hills. More

like mounds, some with gently sloping sides and some with steep sides. All were covered with grass and vines and a few small trees. There weren't many trees, though, and no large ones, which was odd in a world filled with trees that reached almost to the sky.

Beside me, Ralph put down his rifle and stared. "We found it." He stared at the mounds.

"Found what?" Ahead, Noah had turned towards us. He lifted his arms in the universal gesture that said he didn't know what he was looking at and wondered if we did.

"Buildings." Ralph pointed at the mounds. "They've been abandoned long enough for the forest to have taken over to the extent that there's nothing to see except their general outline."

"Are you sure?" I tried to see buildings in the mounds. With a healthy dose of imagination, I could see walls and ceilings behind the dirt and detritus. But it could have been no more than imagination. The mounds could have been just what they seemed at first look. Mounds.

Ralph was sure of his assessment. "I've been on enough expeditions to recognize the outlines of buildings when I see them. And I'm looking at more than one building here. Many more." His stare went from the ocean to the mounds and back. "It's a city and was built on the seashore as cities often are for convenience of transportation or simply because people choose to live near a source of food and enjoyment."

Noah and Midnight came back to join us, and Ralph repeated to him what he'd told me. Noah examined the mounds with that new information in mind and nodded. "I believe you are right."

"We've found what we were looking for. The origin of the portal."

"Or a settlement of beings that didn't survive the primitive stage." The mounds could be covering anything. A sophisticated space station or primitive buildings made of animal skins stretched over branches.

"Let's find out."

Ralph was practical. "We didn't bring the kind of equipment needed to excavate buildings that have been buried for thousands of years by tons of dirt."

"We have one shovel. That's all we need to uncover enough of one building to get a feel for the style and degree of sophistication of the whole place."

So, we dug the shovel out of the trailer where we'd stuck it. I carried Peanut because we didn't want to leave him alone. And we set off for the mounds.

We didn't get far.

Peanut felt it first. He squirmed in my arms. Then he whimpered. Then he tried to jump free. I stopped walking, not because I sensed anything wrong, but because I needed to get a better grip on him. I shushed him and rocked him but nothing worked. He didn't settle back down. Instead, if anything, got worse, crying and looking at me with huge, frightened eyes.

Then something stopped Midnight in his tracks.

His fur rose, he growled low, and he refused to go further. He circled a couple of times, then retreated back towards the beach. Not all the way but far enough to make it clear he wasn't going with us.

"You guys go ahead. I have Peanut and he's becoming a problem. I'll go back to the beach and watch both dogs." I started after Midnight. "I guess they don't like mounds."

Noah regarded the dogs thoughtfully. "Or something nearby is bothering them." He looked around but there was nothing to alarm us. "Dogs have heightened senses. There might be something we don't know about." His rifle had been slung over his shoulder. Now he shifted it so he could hold it casually but ready to use if need be.

Nothing happened other than that the dogs and I headed for the beach. But we didn't go all the way because a few yards into our walk they both quieted down. Peanut curled up in my arms and once more became the snuggle bug we'd come to know, and Midnight's status changed from alert to relaxed.

He slowed and then stopped, turning towards Noah and Ralph though he made no move to rejoin them. But his whole demeanor was one of watchfulness. He was on alert. He was watching for something.

Ralph also unslung his rifle and the two men continued towards the mounds. But now they went slowly, one step at a time and stopping between steps to check their environment. But nothing was out of place.

The birds still sang raucously as if there was nothing wrong.

But something was. We knew it. We felt it.

CHAPTER 18

Step by careful step the men walked towards the mounds. Until Ralph stopped. He put his rifle down and bent over. Something was wrong but I had no idea what. He found a log and sat, propping his rifle next to him where it would be easy to grab if it was needed. Then he rested his hands on his knees and put his head down on his arms. And he sat. And sat.

The dogs and I were still close enough to the men that I could make out Noah's expression. He looked toward me, and we communicated silently, asking what was going on. Because something was, we just didn't know what.

He moved towards Ralph and said quietly, "You stay here, Ralph. I'll check things out a bit and come right back." Ralph nodded with his head still in his hands and Noah proceeded towards the mounds.

But he didn't go far. He was walking slowly, carefully, as before, when he, too, suddenly doubled over. He supported himself with his rifle or he'd have fallen.

He quickly backed away. He was so close to the mound he could have reached out and touched it. But he didn't because he was doubled over in obvious pain. He backed away from the mound until whatever was bothering him disappeared and he was able to stand straight and tall once more.

A few more steps and he'd returned to where Ralph still sat with his head in his arms though instead of looking at our friend Noah looked my way and we silently asked each other what was happening. Because we'd been in enough worlds and had enough bad things happen that we knew something was going on. Something invisible. Silent. Subtle. But very real.

Away from them I felt fine and the dogs were once more comfortable. They'd been the first to be bothered by whatever was happening and I'd retreated with them so perhaps I was okay because I hadn't gotten close enough to whatever was it was to be affected.

Or by whatever was on the ground if that's where it was. There was no way to locate something with no physical component. I was frustrated. I was the only one unaffected so I should be doing something but I had no idea where to even begin to look for the problem because there was nothing to see. Or hear. The only sense it affected was feeling. Pain.

I started toward Noah but I was still holding Peanut and I stopped when both Midnight and Peanut whimpered. They were super sensitive to whatever was out there so I backed off until they were quiet once more. Then I just stood there holding Peanut and watching Ralph and Noah while wishing I could do something.

They got out of the danger zone with difficulty but because both had stopped the moment they realized they were in trouble they were still mobile. When they reached me, we all just stood for a moment while they regained enough strength to be able to continue.

Then we all returned to the four-wheelers, where I deposited Peanut on his bed after making sure he was okay, and we three humans sank to the white sand and just sat without talking until the effects of being near the mounds had worn off enough that they could speak without too much effort. It had been that bad.

"What just happened?" Noah leaned back and considered the soft blue sky as if wondering how it could be so innocent after watching what had just happened in its world.

"Booby traps." Ralph stared at the mounds as if doing so would make them give up their secrets.

"Which means you were right a while back. The mounds are indeed buildings. If not buildings, whatever they are they were built by someone."

"And protected from intruders like us by some unknown force."

Noah tore his gaze from the sky to focus on us. "So what do we do now? What *can* we do?"

I looked at the dogs that needed protection. "We go

home and reconnoiter and we don't return until we figure out what's going on and how to deal with it." As I spoke, I knew that I was the least adventurous of the three of us. But this was one time being cautious was a positive characteristic.

The two men nodded agreement. "We'll return in good time. When Noah and I are once again strong and know what we're dealing with."

"We shouldn't leave this place until we are strong enough to make the trip home safely."

"I want to get home now. I don't want to encounter anything dangerous while I'm too weak to fight."

I said what was going through my mind, pushing everything else out. "I doubt that'll be a problem." I took a deep breath and said what could be the truth behind the strange force that had eviscerated us. "I think Ralph was right when he said this world was designed. It was created to be exactly what the creators wanted it to be. It's not real. It's fake. The whole world is fake."

Ralph shook his head. "You're wrong about it being fake. It's real enough but the reality is similar to the reality of a park that's real but was designed and built to be a place for people to enjoy nature at its best. Think about it. Parks are the real world, the preferred world of their creators, but without any nasty side effects."

"How can anyone create an entire world?"

Ralph shrugged. "How could anyone create a portal to a million other worlds? Any civilization that is capable of such an amazing feat can surely create a single world that's exactly how they want it."

"So, if it's perfect, why aren't they still here?"

"And where did they go?"

"And why did they leave booby traps to protect a place and then not return?"

Ralph, having regained his strength, stood and stretched. "All good questions that we shall probably never know the answers to. But answers aren't always necessary. We don't need answers to be here and know we can return to our own world safely even though we can't read the symbols on the mechanism that controls the portal."

He walked a few steps to make sure he was once again close to his normal self. "The important thing is that we are here even though we don't have all the answers. And I promise that we will find enough answers to this mystery city to be able to do deal with whatever we find."

"How do you propose we do that?" Noah followed his example and walked a bit to make sure his strength was returning. "More importantly, once we make the discoveries you are sure we'll make, what can we do with them?"

I had another thought. "What *should* we do with them? Because whatever they are, they'll be mind-blowing. Unique. The kind of discoveries that will change civilization forever."

Ralph had been on enough expeditions to know the answer to my question. "What we *should* do – what we *will* do -- will be determined by what we find beneath those mounds when we figure out how to approach them safely and dig for whatever treasures they hold that have been well hidden for thousands of years. Perhaps millions of years."

We looked back at the mounds. We all wanted in the worst way to start digging for treasure. But we knew that whatever was protecting them wouldn't let that happen. It wouldn't even let us get close enough to make a wild guess as to what lay beneath the weedy undergrowth that covered everything in a layer thousands or millions of years thick.

So, we packed up and went home. We continued the guard duties we'd worked out on the way there but we were less observant because we now believed it was unnecessary in a safe, created world. We of course kept rifles at the ready in case we were wrong.

But nothing dangerous ever came at us and we reached the portal in two days of hard travel because we were no longer meandering in a leisurely manner, looking for whatever caught our attention. We now had an objective. We were going home.

We didn't stop until we were at my cabin, our de facto headquarters. We unloaded the perishables but left everything else in the four-wheelers to be ready for a return trip to the created world. We'd go back, we knew that, but we didn't know when. After we figured how to disable the booby traps.

But first, we decided in a unanimous decision, we'd take a break. We needed to decompress, to internalize the momentous discovery of the city beneath the mounds, and to relearn what life was like in our tiny part of the universe.

I looked around at the starkly beautiful Wyoming landscape. "I like our world."

"Rattlesnakes and all," Noah added with a grin.

"And cougars and bears." Ralph wore an accompanying smile because it was good to be home. "And snow as high as the eves of my house in winter. And sun so fierce we need sunscreen." Neither Noah nor I disagreed because we, too, were glad to be back in a world we knew and understood.

In what was becoming a habit, Ralph went to be early, and Noah and I parked ourselves on the porch steps with Ralph's coffee and biscuits Noah had made that were wonderful. When he settled down some woman would be fortunate to have him by her side. Not me, of course. But someone who'd like biscuits.

I hoped she'd be nice and decided of course she would be because Noah could have his pick of just about anyone he wanted so of course he'd pick someone nice. Or, realistically, he could have his pick if he lived near those lucky women instead of miles from everywhere on an isolated ranch in the middle of the back country of Wyoming. The thought of that isolation making him less likely to become romantically involved with someone else made me happy. I smiled.

"What's so funny?" He leaned back on his elbows and considered the sky and me.

I reddened. "Nothing." I gulped and looked away. "It's a nice night."

He considered the night. The sky. The darkness. The night birds. "Yes, it is." In a puzzled voice because it was like every other night since I'd moved to Wyoming.

We finished the biscuits with Ralph's homemade jam because, though he was a lousy cook, he made great jelly and jam. "I don't contribute much to the cooking around here."

"You don't have to contribute anything. We're staying at your place and the portal is on your property."

"I can make a mean wedding cake. And my cupcakes add a festive note to any celebration, not to mention that my filled sweet rolls have received excellent reviews in the local paper back home." Not that there was much use for any of those things in the middle of nowhere.

"When I get married, I'll be sure to have you make the cake." He tipped his head. "If I get married."

"You might not?"

He moved slightly until our thighs touched but he still looked at the sky instead of at me. "It's a good institution."

"No current plans?"

" Maybe. Some day. If things work out." Said in short bursts as if each thought was separate from the others and shouldn't be taken any other way.

So, we sat while the stars revolved and it was nice to see familiar constellations and to be able to watch the single moon that we'd seen all our lives that was just the right size and shone down bright white and familiar.

We stayed on the porch steps for a long time, until that moon had completed part of its journey across the sky. Then we went to bed with no further conversation. I wondered what direction our talk would have taken had I pushed it further. But I didn't.

CHAPTER 19

We didn't return to the portal right away because we needed to discuss how to disarm the booby traps that could kill us. So, we discussed. And we thought. And we talked. But that was all that happened. No conclusions. No solutions to the problem.

Noah tried to be realistic. "We need to know what kind of traps were used. How they were made. It's a necessary first step." Problem with that solution was that since they were invisible, we hadn't seen what they were.

Ralph's suggestion was more scientific. "We eliminate all the things we know they are not and what's left must be what they are."

Noah pointed out the flaw with that solution. "We'd have to eliminate everything because we don't know anything."

As for me, I always was a practical person. My inherent practical nature had helped the family bakery business so had been honed to a high degree. "We can't know either of those things – or anything at all -- by staying here and talking. We have to return."

They were unanimous in their feelings about that idea. "No. Never. Don't even think it. We'd just get zapped again."

They politely but firmly said I'd not have made the suggestion if I'd been zapped. I didn't know what it was like. And they were right. So, I went quiet, choosing to let the guys who'd experienced pain take the lead the discussion.

Problem was, they talked just about forever without coming up with a viable solution. So in the end, they agreed to my idea. To return. Because there was no other option.

Ralph spoke with slow, measured, unhappy resignation. "The only way to find out what happened is to experience it all over again and try to figure out what was trying to kill us."

Noah kicked the dirt with a booted toe and sighed. "I don't relish the thought of getting zapped again but it's the only way."

Ralph hunched over and looked slightly sick at the thought of repeating something so painful but remained silent in his assent.

"I volunteer," I said without letting myself think because if I'd have hesitated, I'd have said nothing. "I didn't get zapped. So it's my turn. I get zapped while you two watch and figure out what's happening."

"No!" They shouted as one person. "Don't even think it!"

But I kept at them and by the time the sun went

down they reluctantly agreed that they were more likely to figure things out if I was the one zapped instead of either of them. Ralph because he was a scientist and was trained to think through odd-ball situations and this one qualified. Noah because he was a former Army guy who knew about weapons and booby-traps, which was a previously unknown fact about the guy I was now in love with, and it made him at least a semi-expert in the current situation.

By the time full dark dropped around us they accepted the reality that since I was the only other person on the expedition, I was the logical – and the only -- candidate for getting zapped. Lucky me.

"But you guys better do your stuff fast because I'll be writhing on the ground in agony."

They set me straight. "You won't writhe. It doesn't work like that. And when the pain hits don't stick around. As soon as you feel it you back off as far and as fast as possible."

"You won't have any data to use for research if I turn chicken and run."

Ralph reluctantly agreed. "But don't push it. Turn back while you are physically able to do so." He gave me a look similar to that of a researcher before subjecting a beloved test animal to a potentially deadly bacteria. "I hate that you're doing this. But it's the best idea we have. So, I guess we have to go with it."

Noah touched my shoulder, just touched it, but something about the way his fingers trailed down my arm said how much he hated me being the guinea pig and that knowledge sent a shot of warmth through me.

I met his look squarely and fully and so read the depth of his concern and that made the warmth increase a thousand-fold and spread throughout my body. I didn't dare read the look as love but I greedily took whatever it was because it meant he cared and that was more than I'd expected or hoped for.

He touched me again, then let his hand drop. "We can only hope it works and that we see something we couldn't see when we were busy trying to survive. We didn't stop to notice what was killing us or how it was doing it."

I thought we'd leave for the portal the next day. Instead, Ralph and Noah found all kinds of things that needed doing. As the hours passed, I realized they were deliberately putting off going.

They either didn't want to return to what had tried to kill them or they didn't want to put me through the same thing. Either way I loved them for all those hours of delay even as I was aggravated at time wasted and terrified of what lay ahead.

Our trip, when we finally got going, was pretty much a repeat of our previous trip with one small difference. At Ralph's suggestion, instead of each four-wheeler carrying half the stones so they could become homing beacons if we got lost, we threaded rawhide strips through the holes on three of the stones that we then hung around our necks because this time there was the remote possibility of becoming separated from the four-wheelers because we'd be walking around the mounds. With the stones we'd at least each have a homing device on our body.

Ralph slipped one of the impromptu necklaces around his neck and made sure we did the same. "The stones won't take us back to the four-wheelers if we get lost but if they are compasses that point in the direction of the portal. If the worst happens, we should be able to deduce our location by watching the stones to get the direction of the portal and then we can figure out where the four-wheelers are by dead reckoning.

"We should be able to use that data to create a kind of map and figure where the rest of the team is in relation to the portal. We will be able to find each other."

"What about the dogs?" We'd taken them with us before because we didn't know what else to do with them because the Johnsons were already watching our horses and had several dogs of their own. They didn't need any more.

After considerable discussion we decided to take them with us once again. We made a cage for Peanut in the second trailer so when we left him alone, he'd not be able to jump out and go exploring and get lost. Not that we expected him to do much beyond sleep. He was still bone thin from starvation and pretty much all he did was eat, sleep, and do his business in the bushes.

Midnight, on the other hand, was a valuable

member of our group. Though we no longer expected dangerous animals to threaten the expedition in the artificial world we felt safer knowing he was there with his heightened senses and protective nature. We looked forward to the day when the same would be true of Peanut.

We reached the deserted city in short order because this time we knew where we were going instead of just meandering. We parked the four-wheelers on the white sand beach. We made sure the dogs had plenty of food and water and that Midnight understood that he was to guard the four-wheelers and Peanut instead of accompanying us.

Then we hiked the short distance to the mounds. The guys stood back with concern written all over them while I proceeded slowly and cautiously towards the mounds that had almost killed them.

One step at a time I told myself. One slow step and then another. And another. And so on. I braced myself for whatever might happen, vowing to take the pain as long as I could before retreating so Noah and Ralph could get as much data as possible.

I kept walking. Nothing happened. I walked further. Still nothing happened. I'd been watching my feet to avoid stumbling over the exposed roots and twigs that covered the forest floor so wasn't aware of how far I'd gone. Until I bumped into something. Unable to continue, I glanced up. Whatever it was loomed large inches in front of me.

I'd reached the closest mound, and nothing had happened. No excruciating pain. No writhing on the ground. No bending over because I couldn't stand straight. Nothing.

I looked back at the two men who were watching with mouths open in amazement. "Come on. It's okay." I waved them close.

They looked at me for a long time but they didn't approach. Instead, they conferred. Then they carefully, cautiously repeated my short trip and they did it the way I'd done it. One step at a time, minutely examining their surrounding as they came, pausing when they reached the places where the pain had hit. Then continuing on because there was no pain.

They reached me. Stood on either side of me. Were amazed that they could stand straight and tall without pain. Ralph said it first. "The booby traps are gone."

Noah walked around to make sure he could do so. He returned and just stood. "I don't understand."

The area was strewn with the trappings of an old forest. Trees, old and young, fallen branches in various stages of decay, logs and stumps, some bare and some covered with moss with everything done in the multitudinous shades of brown and green that bespoke a healthy ecosystem.

We found places and sat. I looked around. "What happened? More to the point, what didn't happen and why didn't it? We didn't get zapped. Why not?"

We were all perplexed. It was clear to me that the

men expected to feel pain any second but it never happened. Without their experience of pain, I found myself thinking way ahead of them but I still couldn't wrap my mind around what hadn't happened. "This place is ancient. Thousands of years old if the depth the buildings are buried is any indication." Ralph nodded that they must be at least that old. "So were the booby traps a one-time thing after which they lost power?"

That might explain the difference. I thought back to the first time. I'd watched both men be hit by excruciating pain. I closed my eyes to better picture what had happened and finally said, "That's not it." I opened my eyes to find them watching me with a question on their faces. "Ralph was hit first, then Noah. Noah got farther before he was overcome with pain but not much farther and when the pain hit it was just as bad for him as for Ralph.

"So, the only difference I can see is that Noah is younger and could take more pain before it overcame him. If the power source was diminishing, he wouldn't have been hit as hard. The pain wouldn't have been as intense."

Noah nodded. "I guarantee that it was bad. Couldn't have been any worse."

"So, it's not a lack of power."

I reached for my stone necklace. Fiddling with something while thinking was a habit from childhood I'd never managed to break. When I was really small it had been my hair until my mother cut it short. After that it was anything available.

A plastic ring that had once sealed a bottle. A piece of string. A family brooch my grandmother gave me for my fifth birthday because I'd admired it. Today it was a stone that resembled an opal strung on a strip of rawhide that would double as a homing beacon if I got lost.

"It's warm." I was surprised. "The stone is warm."

CHAPTER 20

Ralph checked his. "Mine too."

Noah held his out. "They are all warm."

"Because they are doing something?"

I don't know who said it. We were all thinking it. "They are preventing whatever caused the pain."

I was the volunteer. I'd sought pain out and been fortunate that it didn't touch me. So, checking the truth of our joint idea was my responsibility.

I removed the stone necklace. I set it on the ground beside me but my fingers lingered on the smooth, warm surface. I wanted to keep touching it. But I didn't. I pulled my hand away and the instantaneous pain doubled me over. I was silent because even moaning would hurt too much. I simply existed in a bubble of sheer agony, the world forgotten.

Noah was beside me in seconds. Or so he said later. I was in too much pain to notice anything. He grabbed the stone and replaced it around my neck. The pain receded but he held me until my body realized it didn't hurt anymore and slowly got past its reaction to the pain itself and I was able to rejoin the world. Mere seconds had passed but had felt like hours. The pain had been that intense.

"You got it the worst of all of us," he said in a quiet voice inches from me. "You were the closest to the mound." He rocked me like a baby. "I'm so sorry."

The pain was gone but the memory lingered. I experimented moving my body and knew I'd be normal again given enough time. "It was pain but that's all it was." I knew that once the men had retreated from the area where the pain was inflicted, they'd not had aftereffects. "It's just pain." If I said it enough times, maybe that would make it true. "It's only pain. A mental thing. Nothing permanent and nothing fatal."

Noah was grim. "After this we keep the stones with us at all times."

I thought of Midnight. "We should put one on Midnight's collar."

"Peanut doesn't have a collar." We decided to make one for him with the remnants of the rawhide we'd used to make our necklaces and as soon as we returned to the four-wheelers, I braided several strands together and made him a makeshift collar with a multi-colored stone where most collars hold a name plate and then I added a stone to Midnight's name plate so they jingled when he moved.

"With the booby traps no longer a threat we can

commence excavating the ruins of what I'm sure will be a fascinating city." Ralph's voice was mild. His excitement was anything but. "Peanut can come too. We'll be staying in one place most of the time so we can bring his bed and he can be near us. As he gets better, he'll become active."

Instead of bringing supplies from the four-wheelers we drove them to the edge of the city and parked them. Peanut remained in his bed in the trailer and watched us work with interest and a face that wondered why humans were working so hard to dig a bunch of holes.

Time had buried the city deep, and roots had made the cover a tangled web. We dug almost five feet of pure brute effort before hitting something solid that turned out to the roof of the closest building, the one I'd bumped into. Or something similar to stone. It was bright red and wasn't stone or cement or anything we recognized but it was as hard as either of them and smooth as glass. Probably harder than stone. After breaking one shovel trying to dent the roof we gave up.

"No sense ruining more shovels. We'd just have to get more and that would take time and we'd be in the same situation when we tried again."

So, we gave up trying to dig through the roof and instead dug along the side until a slice of the building was visible, also bright red and as impenetrable as the roof. "This material has protected what's inside this building for more years than we can imagine."

"I wonder what we'll find when we reach a door."

"If we find one it might be locked."

I touched the stone around my neck. "Something tells me the stones will unlock the doors. They've been the keys to everything else so why not also be the keys to the city?"

Ralph said wishful thinking wouldn't get us anywhere and we returned to digging out the sides of the building in hopes of finding a door or at least a window.

Two days of hard digging later, we found a door. No windows, which was odd, but the door was promising. Except it was locked and the stones didn't open it. "People used the stones to provide for city-wide protection and government type things like going from one world to another. But I suspect they didn't use them to lock their homes because if they did then everyone could access every home. Who'd want that?"

So, we stared at the door and wondered if it would stay shut for the next few thousand years because we didn't know how to unlock it.

Midnight got us in the buildings. Not the building we were trying to access, he found entry into one of the larger ones that was also covered in thousands of years of detritus but not as deeply because of its placement where wind from the nearby ocean had blown enough to keep the accumulation of dirt to a minimum, at least on the side facing the sea.

Actually, it was Midnight's penchant for chasing small animals that got us in when one of the many squirrel-like animals that were everywhere caught his attention. He, of course, chased it. Up and over several mounds and between others until it scampered along the side of what turned out to be one of the largest buildings in the city. One that overlooked the ocean.

The squirrel-like animal scooted into a nest in one of the many tangled vines that had made excavation a nightmare. Midnight went after it. Unable to reach the animal, he dug at the dirt and vines with vigor, thinking he'd reach his prey.

Instead, as we watched, something beneath a thin covering of dirt and detritus moved. It was large – huge -- and slid to one side, leaving a hole that immediately filled with dirt and vines. The squirrel, having lost its nest in the collapse of that part of the mound, scampered to the top of the mound and into a tree where it was safe.

It stared down at our huge dog with what I was sure was derision. Laughter, perhaps. Then it moved from tree to tree along the upper branches until it disappeared from sight, leaving a disappointed Midnight staring at nothing.

We, on the other hand, moved as one person to see what had been uncovered and see what we'd been working for two days to accomplish with no result that Midnight had just handed us. Entry into the city.

"It was the stones. I knew the stones would be the key to unlock the city."

"Midnight has a stone on his collar."

"They didn't unlock the building we dug out and Midnight was with us then, too."

"That was a personal home. There was a desire for privacy. The building that Midnight opened is huge. A commercial or government building of some kind. Such building must have been available to anyone in possession of a stone."

We made short work of clearing the debris that had fallen into what we now knew was a very large doorway, the kind that crowds could pass through with ease, so we could enter and see what this ancient civilization had been like. As soon as we cleared a path wide enough for us to travel single file, we went inside with Midnight following because his prey was gone so he had nothing better to do.

As we entered what resembled a large public foyer, the room lit up. "The mechanics still work." Ralph was in awe. "After thousands of years. What must the level of technology have been to create something that works after all that time?"

"The same technology that created a portal that still works after those same thousands of years. That's what level of technology did it."

"Don't touch anything." Ralph looked around. "We don't want to contaminate anything."

"We also don't want to trip any more traps." Noah stayed carefully away from the walls.

Midnight didn't understand. He moved to the closest wall to give it the sniff test and it, too, lit up like the room itself.

So, we moved close and examined what was now on display. "It's a map of the city."

"Like the maps you find in rest areas on our freeways so you can see where you are and find what you're looking for and then choose the most efficient route to get there."

Ralph stroked Midnight's head. "Good doggie. Excellent doggie." Midnight's tail wagged as he bounded away from Ralph to continue his explorations. We watched him go.

"Should we stop him or let him go?"

"Nothing has harmed any of us so far. I say we follow his lead since I doubt we can stop him anyway." The dog had left the lighted map and was ahead of us, sniffing and looking and generally behaving as though he was in doggie heaven. Which he most likely was as first one display he neared lit up and then another until all the outer walls of the room, a rotunda of sorts, were lit with displays of one kind or another.

"This is an archaeologist's dream." Ralph went from one display to another in a kind of dazed euphoria. "There's a dozen lifetime's of research in this room alone, not to mention the rest of the city. And this entire world."

One display caught his interest. A collection of stones arranged in precise rows and columns with descriptions beside each. "I need a Rosetta stone." He sighed. "Because I still can't read the language."

"You'll figure it out." Noah patted him on the back. "You always do."

"This civilization has defeated me so far and I see no way I'm going to decode the inscriptions we are now surrounded by." Ralph sounded defeated in the midst of the victory of finding what we'd been seeking. "There's a lifetime of learning in this building alone if I can only read what they wrote."

"If there are other buildings that the stones can unlock then we can split up and look for a Rosetta stone."

He cocked his head and straightened somewhat in thought. He wasn't completely upright but enough that he acknowledged the possibility of future success. "Good idea. I doubt it'll lead anywhere but it's worth a try." He looked around. "Though why I'm feeling down when we just stumbled onto the biggest find in human history is beyond me." He tried to stand tall and proud and almost succeeded. "But for some reason, I am."

"Can it be that the sheer vastness of this place is overwhelming?"

I remembered when, as a child, our family bakery received a huge order that could be make-or-break for our business. But even as my parents celebrated, they fell into depression from concern about their ability to fulfill it.

But they accepted the order and what followed was an all-out effort on the part of each family member working harder than ever before. We got the order out in time and the client was pleased. That order put the business on a secure footing. Now Ralph reminded me of my parents at that time.

He thought over what I'd said. "You're right, I'm sure." He straightened the rest of the way until he stood tall, proud and newly energized. "There's a city waiting to be explored so let's get busy."

Before we knew it, Noah and I were following him from room to room as he mentally cataloged the contents for further study. And so, we spent the day, following Ralph and meeting Midnight now and then as he, too, meandered through the building and learned in his own way about the civilization that had created the portal.

When we finished touring the building and returned to the outside world, Ralph turned to us. "Tomorrow, we separate as you suggested. We test all the buildings with the stones until we find three more that open. Then we each become an urban explorer."

"Why go elsewhere? Why not continue what you started? You said there's a lifetime of learning in this one building alone."

He looked at the building we'd just left. "I won't forget this place but there are other places, don't you think?" There was more but he didn't say why he chose to pass up the building we'd left in order to search the larger city. He was looking for something. We just didn't know what.

CHAPTER 21

Midnight went with Noah. As I meandered about alone, I accepted that he'd known Noah longer than me so it was logical he was the preferred human even as I hoped Peanut would someday become 'my' dog. I finally returned to the puppy's bed in the trailer where he was scrambling about with his tail wagging. He was recovering quickly from almost starving, and he was bored.

"Fella, what say you come with me?" His tail wagged so hard his whole body shook as I tried to figure a way to bring him with me because though he was stronger than when we'd found him, he was still weak. The solution was a small cart we'd brought to double as a wheelbarrow if we found anything in need of being hauled.

I transferred Peanut's bed to the cart and then lifted the puppy into it along with some food and water and we set off to see what we could find. His companionship was much appreciated, and he watched the world with interest. It wasn't his birth world. It wasn't even the world we'd brought him to. Our world. It was a third world but he didn't know the difference.

We checked out several mounds that remained locked. Most likely private residences. The door to the fourth mound opened when we were close enough for the stones to sense the building and slide the door open. It took some effort to clear a path through the debris that fell into the opening so I could pull the cart through but eventually I stepped inside. As in the first one, the lights went on the instant I crossed the threshold.

It didn't take long to figure out the building's purpose. It was a resort which made sense for a city close to the seashore. It was round, like the first building, but had suites all around the outside and a small lobby. Each suite had a door that opened out the back onto what had undoubtedly been lush gardens at one time. Several thousands of years ago.

A lot of those back doors opened as Peanut and I entered the rooms and a lot of dirt fell into the openings and blocked their ability to close. I'd have to tell the guys. We should dig the doors free of dirt so they could close and continue to protect the insides.

In one suite when that outer door opened, instead of a pile of dirt, I saw sunlight beyond with just a thin layer of dirt that could easily be swept away. I could walk through it and be outside as those long-ago inhabitants had undoubtedly done and enjoy a gorgeous view of the ocean.

As I stood in the doorway and inspected the room, I realized I could see through the wall. The entire wall. Which answered the question of why we hadn't found any windows in the previous building. Whoever built the city hadn't needed them. They'd been able to look through the walls.

"Well, hello." Noah peered through the sparse vines hanging over the open doorway. "I heard a commotion and came to see if you were in trouble."

"No trouble. You heard dirt falling from doors opening."

"Must have been lots of doors."

"It was." I explained about digging them free of dirt so they could be closed, and he agreed. He was outside, I was inside. We looked at each other and I thought about the see-through walls. "Can you see through the wall from where you stand?" I'd not want people to see me if I was inside so perhaps they were the alien equivalent of one-way glass. But who knew what the beings who built the city were like. Perhaps they hadn't valued privacy.

He didn't know what I was talking about but he stepped back and checked the part of the wall no longer covered in rubble. "Nope. Can't see a thing except that it's baby blue and is pretty dirty now and made of the same stuff as the first building. Why?"

"Come inside and you'll see."

He picked his way through the dirt in the open doorway and joined me and then turned to look back at the opening. "Oh, my goodness. One way glass." He thought over his words. "Or one-way whatever this stuff is."

"We should tell Ralph. He'll want to know. And about digging the other doors clear of debris."

Yes, we should." Noah examined the room and the ocean view through the transparent wall and the open doorway. "But there's no hurry."

He looked at the ocean again and then turned to me. I couldn't read his thoughts but was sure his mind was racing. Thinking about something. His eyes shuttered the way they did sometimes because he didn't want me knowing his thoughts though I could never hide mine from him.

He took my hand in one of his while grabbing Peanut's cart with the other and pulled us both through the open doorway. "I have an idea if it's okay. This is a nice place from which to enjoy the view and I'm declaring a work break because we need and deserve one." With which he pulled a couple of what could have been chairs through the doorway and sat us down facing the limpid blue ocean.

He plopped himself on one of the maybe-chairs and let out a sigh. "This must be a resort. Whoever built it painted it the same light blue color as the ocean – good marketing ploy -- and the interior is gorgeous and comfortable." He looked around at the vines and other weeds. "And this was once probably a lovely garden."

"I had the same idea. It's a resort."

"So, let's take advantage of what this resort has to offer." He stretched his legs out in front of him, leaned back, gave a long, comfortable sigh, and looked at me with one eye because he'd have to turn his head to look at me full on and that would have required too much effort. "Do you agree?"

"Absolutely." He was so close and so gorgeous that I could barely speak. I croaked instead.

"Is something wrong?" He sat up straight and was suddenly, totally alert. He looked at me. Really looked. With alarm. "You sound funny. Are you in pain? Are the stones not protecting you?" His whole being showed concern and I wanted to die from embarrassment.

With great effort I cleared my throat and managed to speak normally. "No. Nothing's wrong."

He relaxed again. "Good. I was worried for a moment."

"No worries." I squelched a squeak that threatened to put the lie to my words.

I dropped into the second chair, and we sat for a long time watching the waves break on the beach and the sun move across the sky accompanied by the three moons that revolved on their unknowable schedule. I said nothing because I didn't want to make any more gaffes but I didn't know why Noah was quiet. My gaze left the ocean and turned stealthily in his direction to see if everything was alright.

I nearly jumped out of my skin because my gaze

met his. He was looking at me instead of the ocean. Straight at me. Full on. Staring. "What's wrong?" I felt my face, checked my clothes, wiggled my body. I was normal. "Why are you staring?"

He moved millimeters but stayed facing me. "Because looking at you is enjoyable. More enjoyable than looking at the ocean, lovely as it is." But he returned to watching the waves move across white sand. "Sorry. I won't do it again. I didn't know it bothered you."

"It doesn't!" I shouldn't have shouted, shouldn't have spoken so quickly. I definitely didn't want him to get the wrong idea. Or the right one. That I loved having him watch me. "I mean – You can watch – I mean – It's okay – Sort of – " I gave up and stopped talking completely.

"Really?" He moved. Twisted and looked away from the beach so as to once more be looking towards me. Turned his chair slightly to make the looking easier and more comfortable as befitted someone on vacation. "Then I'll continue to do so."

A slow movement passed through his body, top to bottom, and he sank even deeper into the chair which had a hard surface, thank goodness, because anything soft would have disintegrated a few thousand years earlier and we'd be sitting on dust. But the chairs conformed to our bodies. Of course, they did. Any civilization capable of creating portals to other worlds could easily make a comfortable chair that would last forever. And we were the recipient of that technology.

He wiggled once more and then sighed in contentment. "A restful chair and a wonderful view." There was no mistaking what view he was referring to. Me. I turned red. Then redder. Then I twisted uncomfortably as my body grew warmer with the beginning of a frisson of excitement coursing through me. And he started to grin at my obvious embarrassment and that made things even worse.

How well did he read my body language? He was the most perceptive person I'd ever met. He might know what I was thinking and know that I was in love with him. He probably did. I sank further into the hard soft chair but was unable to sink into it completely.

Noah, on the other hand, wasn't in the least uncomfortable. And, as usual, that awareness of his surroundings that was such a core part of him, told him things I couldn't begin to guess about the day and the long-dead city we were exploring. And about me.

I hoped not me but was pretty sure he was reading me like a book because it was what he did and that made me feel even worse and wish even harder that I could sink even deeper into the hard-soft chair.

I contemplated a future of constant embarrassment because of that ability of his and I'd just have to get used to it. As I was wiggling in embarrassment, sure he was reading my feeling easily, he spoke. "It's not going to happen."

"What's not going to happen?" I tensed. Turned

away because maybe then he couldn't read me so easily. But I watched him from the corners of my eyes.

He slumped still deeper into the hard-soft chair and pulled his hat down over his eyes but I could see the smile that threatened to fill his entire face. What was he smiling about? What was so funny? "Whatever you're thinking, it's not going to happen." He lifted the hat enough that I could see laughing eyes. "Never. Not ever."

"What are you talking about?"

"You." He shifted enough to sit straighter but his look never left me. "You. Me. What you were getting into such a tizzy about just now. Which must be interesting. Very interesting." He sat up as straight as possible, reminding me of Ralph when he'd forced himself to stand to his full height after being zapped because doing so was important, a reminder to himself as to why he was here. "What I'm talking about is you and me together. Us. Whatever you're thinking about a lonely future for the two of us – and I'm sure that's what you're thinking, absolutely positive it's what you're thinking -- is not going to happen."

"Us?" Could he possibly understand me over the squeak in my voice?

"Yep. Us. As in two people together. That, on the other hand, ought to happen. Should happen. Will happen."

"Oh." What else could I say? Nothing.

Then he pulled his hat down over his eyes again

and dropped back in the chair and folded his arms over his waist and I grew furious. How dare he be so at ease when I was practically jumping out of my skin!

Before I could talk myself out of it, I stood up and crossed the tiny space between our chairs. I didn't know what I was going to do but I was going to do something. Something awful. Something horrible. Something to make him regret that comfortable smile. Maybe I should slap him upside the head like my parents always threatened to do to us kids and never did but the threat got our attention. Every single time.

Except I didn't have time to do anything because when I reached his chair he moved. Quickly. Laughing as he moved. Tossing his hat to the ground he grabbed me and pulled me onto his lap.

It was exactly where I wanted to be and would have been heaven if I was there for a purpose other than making him sorry he was born. So, I fought him while trying to think of something other to do than slapping him because suddenly I didn't want to do that or anything remotely similar. That is, I started to fight him. I meant to fight him.

But I didn't have time because, before I got my body fully charged, he pulled me close and kissed me. Just like that. No warning, no 'pretty please.' He just did it. And I kissed him back because it felt good. Right.

When the kiss ended, I lay on top of him in that warm sunshine and stared at his face which was mere inches from mine. "Why are you smiling?"

He pulled me closer if such was possible. "I'm smiling because I've been waiting for this to happen for a long time." Then the content look disappeared, and an alarmed look spread across that formerly happy face. "Unless you didn't want it. Then of course I'll stop. If you want me to stop."

The look grew more alarmed. "Is it? Do you want me to let go now and leave you alone forever? Because if that's what you want then that's what I'll do." He pushed me away a bit. Enough to see me clearer. "Did I read you wrong all this time? Do you dislike me?" After a moment, he added, "Instead of loving me like I thought you did? Like I love you?"

I collapsed back onto his body because it was absolutely the most perfect place to be and he blew out a big sigh. "Whew!" He wrapped me in his arms. After a few moments, he continued. "I did read you right after all. Thank goodness because it would be endlessly difficult if I was in love with you and you didn't return the feeling."

I did the only thing I could think of at the moment. I kissed him and he kissed me back. And we sat like that for a long time watching the waves on that alien beach and listening to alien birds in an alien sky with Peanut enjoying everything about the day and we did it together and knew we'd be doing it exactly that way for years to come.

CHAPTER 22

Eventually we decided to do a bit more exploring. "It's why we are here, and we know what this building is so we should continue on and make other discoveries. Get the city figured out."

"We can only enter public buildings."

"There must be enough of them to tell the story of this city if not of the whole civilization."

So, we moved. I left his lap, we grabbed Peanut's cart and set off to find another building to explore so we could honestly tell Ralph we'd been doing our jobs instead of loitering.

We shortly found another public building easily because the public buildings were the largest mounds. We walked around it until the earth moved and crumbled, indicating there was a door that had slid open. All we had to do was remove the dirt that had fallen into the opening, and we could enter and find out what kind of building it was.

Peanut watched with interest and yipped his

approval when we pulled his cart through another very wide doorway and into a large open building. The entire building was one vast room with bleacher type seating all around and a clear central area that gave no indication what it was used for. "It has seating for spectators."

"An arena?"

"Or something similar."

There wasn't much to see. There were smaller rooms equipped only with a few tables and chairs with cabinets all along the walls beneath the bleachers along. There were four large entrances that divided the building into fourths. A spotlight shone on the center of the floor. "An opera house?"

"Then what are the small rooms for?"

"Practice? Changing rooms? Strategy sessions for sports teams?"

We wandered all around pulling Peanut as we went and found nothing different about any of it. It was a large auditorium of some kind. "Maybe Ralph will recognize its purpose. It might be similar to the excavations he's helped with."

"Maybe." Noah had his doubts as we left the building the way we'd come and went in search of Ralph. "It's mostly a big empty space."

We found Ralph in another large public building in a state of excitement. "I've found what's close to the holy grail." This building was the opposite of the one we'd left. Where our find was one large room, Ralph's was a warren of small rooms, each different from the others.

We asked what made it so interesting. It was just a bunch of little rooms as far as we could see but Ralph was confident that it was of supreme importance. "It's not the holy grail itself, not the most important building in this civilization but it's the next best thing. It's a museum. Or a library. A place where this civilization stored their knowledge."

He pulled us eagerly from one room to another. "Each room describes a different facet of the civilization. It's a treasure trove." There were rooms showing technology our scientists were only dreaming of. One showed spaceships. Another showed portals that made those ships obsolete. Still another one had transportation devices that skimmed the ground without disturbing it that made automobiles obsolete and there were more with medical devices we could only guess the functions of. "It'll take years to classify the things in just half of this building let alone deconstruct them to learn how they work."

His face gleamed. "Even without the holy grail, this building did one thing." He pulled his collar loose and indicated a bare neck. "No necklace. No stone because I don't need protection. With the information in one of these rooms, I deactivated the booby traps."

"How?"

"One room was all about the stones, including how to deactivate the city's protective shield. I couldn't read the instruction manual but I could figure how to deactivate the shield from the pictures."

We cautiously removed our necklaces. Nothing happened. "This is wonderful."

"It'll take exploring the city to a whole new level."

Noah had a question. "With all the information here why isn't it this building the holy grail?"

"Because I still can't decode their system of writing. All I can do is surmise things from the illustrations. I need a Rosetta stone to teach me how to read the fine print. I guessed about the stones, and I guessed right. A Rosetta stone will eliminate guesswork."

"We'll find it."

He sighed. "I hope so."

We explained about our own find. "Not as exciting as a library but it's an odd building. Want to take a look?"

He said he did, and we returned to the large, one room building pulling Peanut behind us. When we entered and the lights lit up the huge place, he was suitably impressed. "Whatever it is, it's magnificent. I'd guess it's an amphitheater."

It took mere minutes to show him the building in spite of its size including a tour of the small rooms beneath the bleachers after which we returned to the main room.

He looked around. "I wonder what the view is like from the bleachers." Without waiting for us, he began climbing the stairs between the rows of seats and we followed. And then it happened.

A cone of light appeared in the center of the empty floor. We turned to turn to see what was happening. I watched uneasily as the cone of light dimmed and a man appeared in the center. He was dressed in odd clothing but he was definitely human. "This place was created by humans."

"The portal allowed people to travel among worlds."

Ralph considered the man in the middle of the huge room. "It's a hologram, of course," He said in a whisper so as not to interfere with what the man was saying. "But it's so real I feel I can touch it."

The hologram spoke. We listened in rapt silence until we realized we couldn't understand a word. As we listened anyway, Ralph said, "I need that Rosetta stone. I want to understand what he's saying."

We dropped into seats in the huge amphitheater and listened. I did so out of respect because the holographic man was wrapped in an aura of dignity. Even Peanut grew quiet. I didn't know why Noah and Ralph also listened but I suspected they, too, were awed by the holographic presence.

The man spoke for a minute or so and then stopped as if waiting for something. "What does he want?" We didn't know because we didn't know the language. Then the hologram began all over and repeated its speech. Then it waited once more for our response. When none came, it repeated its speech still again.

We left the bleachers and the hologram disappeared. "It's on automatic. It appears whenever someone is in the bleachers and will repeat its speech until it gets a response."

"Then what will happen?"

"I don't have a clue."

Ralph paced back and forth with his hands behind his back until he stopped in mid stride. "I want to check something out." Without another word, he headed for the closest room beneath the bleachers. We followed.

He ignored the table and chairs, choosing instead to open one of the cabinets along the wall. A smile spread across his face as he inspected the contents and he said, "Bingo."

"Bingo?"

"I found it. The holy grail."

"A Rosetta stone? The stuff in the cabinet is a Rosetta stone?" All I saw was a bunch of tablets similar to a small laptop.

"This building is a school or this civilization's equivalent, and these rooms are the classrooms. The hologram is the teacher." His smile spread until happiness engulfed his entire body. "All I need to do is take out a packet of information from one of these cabinets, choose which packet of information I wish to learn, and take it to the main room."

"You still can't understand the language so what

good will that do?"

"I'm sure that somewhere in one of these rooms I'll find a packet that will teach me their language." He closed the cabinet door and turned to us. "Because surely there were many languages among a civilization that covered much of the universe. Surely people from different places needed to learn other languages and this is where they came to learn them."

"It's the key to this civilization."

There was nothing more to say. We trooped back to the four wheelers to let what we'd found sink in and to give Peanut a chance to do his business in the grass along the beach and to make sure Midnight was still around and not getting into trouble.

We removed the stones from their collars because they weren't needed. And as the sun set and the three moons continued their gyrations around the sky, we made a campfire and talked about the future. But what we'd discovered was so momentous that we decided it would take a long time to come to a decision as to what to do with our discoveries.

The next morning, we made sure the city was intact and all the buildings were closed and safe from the elements. This involved a full day of shoveling dirt away from the open doors in the resort so the doors could close but in time the city was once more safe from intruders though the only danger we could see was the numerous squirrel-like animals and the ever present birds that flew through trees and swooped overhead almost constantly.

We spent another night along the white sand beach. The following morning, we packed everything back in the four-wheelers and went home.

CHAPTER 23

Being home was anticlimactic. We weren't the same people who'd passed through the portal a few days earlier. We were irrevocably changed. But the world around us on that warm summer day, the world we knew and had believed to be the only one humans could live on, was the same as it had always been. Nothing different at all. So, we felt odd.

Noah made biscuits. Ralph made black, strong coffee. I cooked eggs and sausage. We filled our plates and took them onto the porch where we ate without talking because none of us knew quite what to say. Where to start.

When we finished, we dropped to sit on the steps, that place Noah and I had spent so much time watching the stars, talking, and falling in love. I now knew that's what we'd been doing though I'd not known it at the time. He sat beside me and wrapped an arm around me.

Ralph noticed and said nothing though his eyebrows rose a bit before resuming their rightful place.

He brought a chair from the porch to the ground so he could sit comfortably while still being at eye level with us. "My old knees feel better when I sit in a chair. You two can have the stairs." He started to say something else that I was sure would be about Noah and me being a couple but changed his mind though I thought I saw a glimmer of delight and possibly amusement in his expression.

After a long time, Noah spoke. "Well guys, we're home. We found the Rosetta stone and the civilization it will unlock. So, what's next?"

The flood gates had been opened. Ralph spoke first. "The discoveries waiting for us are what's next. The knowledge. The sheer volume of advanced technology that will change the world forever. It's mind boggling."

"I added my thought. "We must tell someone." We all went quiet, and no one spoke for a long time as we three considered the implications of giving the world the amazing things we'd seen. "Or not tell anyone. Maybe the world isn't ready for what we'll find." They both nodded slightly.

"The technology in that other . Think what it'll mean. Wars will be easier. More people could be killed with greater efficiency."

"We can't let that happen." There was no need to ask each of us how we felt because we all agreed. "But surely all that advanced technology can also help people. Can save lives. Can make lives easier."

"If it doesn't fall into the wrong hands."

"How do we make sure it doesn't?"

"Every new invention has had the potential for both good and evil. Sometimes good won, other times evil did."

Noah asked again. "So, what do we do now? How can we keep the good without also keeping the bad?"

I knew the answer. As the oldest of five kids, I'd learned a thing or two growing up. "We get sneaky. When someone asks how we know what we know we smile and pretend not to know what they are talking about. We learn to tell little white lies without blinking. With a little practice it'll be as natural as breathing." I thought back to all the things I'd done growing up. "It'll be easy. You'll see."

Noah didn't get it. I asked, "Were you an only child?" He nodded. "Then trust me. I know what I'm talking about."

Ralph was ahead of us both. "I have friends in academia. Lots of friends."

"What difference does that make?"

"New discoveries generally come from academia. I know people who will be happy to sneak a little of the knowledge we are about to learn into their own work and thus let it disseminate throughout the academic world and then into everyday life."

We thought about it. "It could work."

"It will work." Ralph examined us from his chair. "But first I believe there are a couple things that should be taken care of.”

“Such as?” Learning the language of that other civilization? Cataloging what we found in the city?

That wasn’t what he was thinking of. “I should move closer to the portal. Commuting from Whitehall to another world on a regular basis will get old fast.” He took in my cabin. “Emma, you are a great hostess but this place is a bit crowded with all three of us here.”

Then, with his eyes crinkling, he added, “I suspect it’ll be just fine for you two, at least until your family grows if you choose to have children, but I prefer a place of my own.”

As Noah and I jumped apart and then came back together because there was no reason to pretend we weren’t a couple, he continued. “But you, Emma, own the property that holds the portal and the surrounding area and you, Noah, own the property with the only other access to it. So would either of you consider selling me an acre or two so I can build a smallish house somewhere closer?”

We talked for hours during which time Noah offered his place for Ralph to live. It was small, the right size for a single person, and the barn could be converted into a workshop. We could bring artifacts from the other world and use the barn to study them.

Noah pulled me still closer. “If we both live here then my place will be available.”

“You have horses.” Those things I still wanted to learn to ride that had almost got me killed.

"We can build a barn here. There's enough room." Acres of room. Many, many acres. I didn't even know how large Uncle Cantrell's ranch was. I made a mental note to find out.

Ralph decided to also keep his town house. "It'll be handy for when my friends visit to pick up the latest technology that they'll distribute to the world. No reason for them to know where it comes from."

"They'll wonder."

"My reputation is such that they'll not ask because they know I'll not tell them."

We eventually built a bridge over the river so Ralph could use it when going to the portal from what had been Noah's cabin and was now his. No horse required.

We built a barn next to the shed behind my cabin that was twice the size of the one at his old place because Noah really did like horses and because I truly did want to learn to ride. Then we built a sturdy corral that no horse could possibly break out of so I could practice riding without any chance of another stampede. Noah made sure of that and didn't laugh once when he tested the fenceposts to make sure they were deep enough and strong enough to make even me feel safe.

Someday I'll learn to ride like a real cowgirl. In the meantime, the four-wheelers get a heavy workout because I'm in that other world more than I'm in the one I was born in. I've come to love that advanced city that we were slowly digging out from under thousands of years of detritus and learning more and more about it with each and every visit.

We do find time to visit other worlds than the one that holds the key to the portal. They are fascinating and give a hint as to what the builders of the portal were like because once Ralph decoded their language, he could follow their travels through the universe, and we replicated many of those journeys. Thus, we learned what they looked for in other worlds. Which ones they preferred. How very much like us they were.

But we never knew where they came from originally. Or where they went when they left that city.

My family went overboard when Noah and I got married. All four of my siblings helped in one way or another and the cake was amazing. Of course, it was. It was made with love.

EIPLOGUE

"Shhh." Noah **held** up a hand for silence. I moved close, urging Cutie Pie forward while trying to avoid small branches that might make noise. I peered over the dead tree we were hiding behind. It was huge and must have been over a hundred feet tall before a storm blew it over.

Now it lay on the forest floor and the root ball that had been torn from the ground was large enough to make perfect cover for us even on horseback. The pack of wild dogs that was about a hundred feet away wasn't the reason for our visit to this world. But there they were, and we didn't want to antagonize them. So, we spied on them from behind that root ball.

We were there to reassess using the horses while exploring other worlds. Our first trial had ended in disaster but since then I'd become a better rider and the horses had been trained to ignore dangerous distractions. Such as the pack of wild dogs we'd unexpectedly encountered.

And the dogs were dangerous, no doubt about that. All the packs of huge wild dogs in that world could easily rip us to shreds in seconds if they thought we were the enemy. Most of the time, though, they ignored us because we were aliens in their world, and they didn't recognize us as anything. We hoped this particular pack would be like that.

I examined the pack, looking for signs it knew we were there and saw nothing, which was encouraging. Then I looked beyond it and saw the puppy. It was the runt of the litter and had been shoved aside as were all runts in this world, pushed from their mother's life-sustaining milk. As Midnight had been. As Peanut had been before we rescued him.

"It's going to die."

"This fate of all runts in this world."

"We have to save it."

Noah pulled back from watching the pack and urged Hazy close to me. He controlled his horse with his knees. I admired that ability. Someday I hoped to do the same but that day wasn't yet. I took his hand, glad once more for this singular man I lived, loved and worked with in a relationship I'd not thought possible until he came along.

He whispered so as not to alert the pack to our presence. "We already have two dogs from this world. Two runts that were rescued." Midnight and Peanuts, all grown up and part of our family.

"It'll die. It's already gaunt and listless." The pup

lay still, watching the mother with longing but not moving towards her because it knew what would happen if it tried. It would be killed.

"I know." He slanted a look towards me that said he knew how much I cared about the pup I'd not known existed until that moment.

We were going to do our best to rescue the pup. Noah's demeanor said he accepted my need to save it. He sighed. "I hope we don't see any more runts on the verge of starvation. How many puppies can we save? How many can we bring back to our world before the vet gets too inquisitive about dogs the size of small horses?"

"This puppy will make three. That's not a lot."

"I guess not." He sighed again and examined the puppy as closely as possible from a distance. "It looks marginally healthy. Enough to survive if we can retrieve it."

"So, what's the plan?" Because Noah always came up with a plan. It was one of his strengths. That and the uncanny awareness of his surroundings that had gotten us out of more than one scrape.

He looked around, thinking how to rescue the pup. We'd chosen the world with the dog packs to try the horses again because we knew it better than most and because of its forests. Less chance of a stampede with trees blocking the way. But we hadn't expected to see a pup in need of help.

He scowled. "I don't know how the horses will

react with an over-sized puppy along for the ride."

"You take the pup on Hazy." Because he was the better horseman. If the pup spooked Hazy, Noah could control him and keep him on course, not to mention calm him down later. I was too new of a rider to do any of those things well. "You be ready and waiting on Hazy. I'll get the pup and hand it to you. Then you head for the portal, and I'll follow on Cutie Pie."

He didn't like that idea. "Too dangerous. The puppy is on the opposite side of the pack from us. We'll have to circle around to reach it and that will surely alert them to our presence. When you go for the pup, they might attack." Our looks met. "I don't want to lose you to a bunch of wild dogs."

"It's a chance I'm willing to take." The puppy was alone and starving because the others had pushed it away from food and warmth. They had their mother. Noah and I had each other. The puppy had no one.

Noah couldn't think of a better plan so after checking the horses to make sure they were ready to run if a fast getaway proved necessary, we rode as quietly as possible in a large circle around the pack.

The pack heard us and went on alert. They watched us circle around them. They made no move in our direction but their ears were flat and their teeth were bared.

Noah led on Hazy. The wild pack watched. They were almost as big as Hazy and could take a horse down easily if even two of them ganged up on him.

Hazy seemed to know this and tried not to move in the direction of the pack but Noah convinced him to get close to the pup. I followed and dismounted as quietly as possible.

Behind Hazy, I was hidden from the pack. I dismounted and quickly scooped up the lethargic pup and handed it to Noah. The pack saw the movement.

They rose, growling low as they went on heightened alert. I mounted Cutie Pie. We backed the horses away from the pack, planning to repeat our circle around them. Then we'd get out of there.

We were barely halfway around the circle when the pack attacked. With a howl that set our teeth on edge the leader started towards us, teeth bared and snapping, ears back, its entire body the personification of aggression.

"Let's get out of here!" Noah kicked Hazy into a gallop, and I did the same on Cutie Pie. Soon the horses were running for their lives, dodging trees and jumping logs in their eagerness to get away from the deadly pack. Noah wanted to slow down and let me go first so he could protect the rear but I motioned him to keep going because he had the pup and holding it made riding more difficult.

Even though it was the runt of the litter it was three times the size of a normal puppy. Hazy could barely carry both Noah and the pup while avoiding trees that appeared before him in confusing rapidity.

"Keep going!" I screamed at Noah and reluctantly

he sped up and soon Hazy was far ahead. As I urged Cutie Pie to greater and still greater speed, I chanced a look back to see how close my pursuers were.

I saw huge, black eyes filled with hatred and blood lust. The leader of the pack was closing in. Soon he'd catch up to Cutie Pie and then it would be all over. I tried frantically to think as a terrified Cutie Pie found another ounce of speed and ran still faster.

She ran so fast that trees blurred as we passed. She ran flat out, and I feared she'd run into something and we'd both die. But the alternative was to be torn to pieces by a pack of wild dogs, so I loosened the reins and let her run.

She knew where the portal was, she knew it represented home and she was following Noah and Hazy who were far ahead. But the pack, led by the leader who was almost at Cutie Pie's flanks, was closing in.

The portal was in view and Noah was almost there. He pushed Hazy into an additional burst of speed, and they went through. At least they were safe. I didn't know if I'd live or die but he and the pup would live. That was one good thing and would have to be enough if the pack caught me and the worst happened. I'd have saved one puppy's life and Noah would also live.

As the leader caught up with Cutie Pie and prepared to attack, I saw a commotion at the portal and tore my eyes from the wild dog long enough to see what was happening. Noah, still on Hazy, was returning. He no longer carried the puppy. Instead, he held two thirty-thirty rifles. He came abreast of me and literally threw one of the rifles at me while bringing the other to his shoulder.

Galloping full speed towards the leader of the pack, he aimed and pulled the trigger in one motion. He hit his target. The shot wasn't fatal, and the monster dog kept coming but a trail of blood sprayed everywhere and it ran slower. The rest of the pack caught up and then passed it, coming for me as Noah tried to rein in Hazy enough to get a second shot. But Hazy had the bit in his teeth and wouldn't be slowed.

I wasn't good enough to both ride and shoot. I was sure of that. But I tried. I pulled the trigger. I didn't hit any of the wild dogs but the sound of my shot, along with several by Noah in rapid succession made them slow and then pause.

They milled about. Their leader was wounded and lagging, they'd heard a sound they'd never heard before and didn't understand. They were unnerved. We took advantage of the momentary pause and urged the horses to run still faster through the portal and into our own world and safety.

Ralph was waiting on the other side of the portal with the puppy in his arms. He didn't even blink when we burst through at full speed. Instead, he merely stepped aside and watched with interest as we galloped past and let the horses slow down. When they were reasonably quiet and had circled back, he waited for us and whatever story we'd have to tell. Because he knew there'd be one. There always was.

But first we found milk for a puppy that took it eagerly. Then Ralph turned to me. "This one's a girl so I think she'll be your dog. Your friend for many adventures." I took the pup and we connected. Female to female. Friend to friend. I hugged her as she chugged milk and wiggled a bit in response to my hug. Yes, we'd make a team.

Noah came behind me and wrapped his arms around me and the pup. Together because we were a package. He didn't speak. He didn't have to. I leaned back into him, and we both luxuriated in the feel of each other and the knowledge that we were alive and safe and the sun was warm and the Wyoming countryside spreading out around us was beautiful and was home.

Then we all returned to the cabin that had become the de facto headquarters of our other world explorations. We were now a cohesive group, a three-person team bringing one invention after another to the world without anyone knowing where they originated. There was always speculation about the source of the new thing that would benefit mankind. None of the guesses were even close.

We put the horses in the barn and made sure the new pup was fed still more milk and that both Midnight and Peanut were outside happily chasing squirrels and investigating all sorts of things that we couldn't see.

Then we went inside with the new pup and just sat. It took a while to get past what had happened but we knew we'd make it because we always did. And we always would. Just like we always brought things back with us.

Sometimes we brought back experiences. Sometimes things. Like one huge puppy that was a runt in its world and a behemoth in ours. That puppy would live a long, happy life because we'd stepped through the portal and been in the right place at the right time.

The new pup whimpered, and I went to see if it needed anything. It did. It needed love so I picked it up and it nestled between Noah and me as we considered the spread sheet Ralph had created of the few worlds we knew out of the millions of worlds out there. And we discussed which one we'd visit next.

THE END

Hi,

I'm Florence Witkop and I hope you enjoyed 'Star Portal.'

If you'd like to sample another of my stories, the following is the beginning of my next novel, 'Talk To Me.'

It's the story of two people who were in the wrong place at the wrong time and ended up being chased by people who want to capture them and experiment on them. Because what happened to them was unusual. Unique. Scary. And important.

It'll be published by Winged Publications in the coming months, will be available on Amazon, and will be free with Kindle Unlimited.

TALK TO ME

by

Florence Witkop

CHAPTER 1

I was in no hurry. Maybe I should have been. If I'd been in a rush to outfit myself with new rain boots because my old ones had holes in them and there was rain in the forecast and if I'd straight to the city to get those boots instead of stopping to enjoy the view – well, if that had been the case, then none of it would have happened. But it was morning, and I had all day so I didn't go straight to the city.

Even so, if the strange wind hadn't chosen that moment to come up the canyon, then there'd still have been no problem. But it came, seemingly out of nowhere, and there was nothing I could do when it came except try to survive.

I'd turned off the highway into the familiar rest area with an overlook so gorgeous that every time I went past, I stopped and while I was there, at the overlook, it took my breath away. Always. Every single time.

The overlook jutted over a long, deep but narrow

valley of pristine wilderness intertwined with the tributaries of a whitewater river that dropped to the valley floor over a series of waterfalls that shot white foam against a green forest backdrop. It was at the top of a funnel formed by the valley that always sent at least a breeze from the bottom to the overlook. Sometimes a strong wind but even on hot days with no wind at all that overlook was comfortable. Cool and delightful.

The only thing in the valley not created by nature was some kind of building at the bottom but it had been well designed and was a color that blended perfectly with the surrounding flora. Most people didn't even notice it and the only reason I did was because I lived not far away and had been contacted by protesters trying to prevent it from being built.

I'd not cared one way or another as long as it didn't interfere with my enjoyment of the area and the builders had been very careful about that, though I did end up on the protest group's hate list for not caring enough about what they considered a desecration of nature. Besides, they'd said, no one knew what that building would be used for. Their expressions had been ominous.

I'd laughed after they left because all I cared about was whether the view was still gorgeous after the building was erected. And it was. I stopped every chance I got, and that day was no exception.

Once parked, I headed for the well-marked path to the overlook. It was a rather long path and went upwards at a steep enough angle to leave me breathless when I arrived, but the view was worth it and I always stayed long enough to catch my breath before the return walk.

That day there was someone else already there if the ancient, dented pickup truck in the parking lot when I arrived belonged to a fellow lover of overlooks. It was old, really old, and I expected to find an equally old person at the end of the trail.

Instead, I saw a man several years older than me with the look about him that current and former military types can't seem to avoid. The posture. The bearing. The short hair. So it wasn't an elderly man. Instead, it was most likely a man who liked antique vehicles and hadn't gotten around to restoring his but was using it for transportation until he got around to doing the actual work.

I checked him out further. Yes, he was definitely military, from the top of his super short haircut to the bottom of his neat and shiny boots. He'd been blessed with an excellent physique that now held a ramrod stiff posture and he had a calculating way of looking at everything and everyone, including me, as I joined him at the railing. But neither of us spoke. Until the silence grew awkward and I said, "Beautiful, isn't it?"

He nodded. Encouraged, I continued. "I love to stop here when I'm going somewhere. Anywhere." I took a breath and continued because he seemed to be listening though he didn't move and barely acknowledged my presence. "You'd think I'd get tired of the view, especially since I'm local and drive by here frequently. But I never do."

"It's awesome." Said without turning from the forest spreading below like a carpet of a thousand different shades of green. But he did answer. He did know I existed.

So, I decided to continue and be friendly. "Are you local too?"

"Just passing through," he replied, finally turning enough to acknowledge my existence.

Then he turned back to the view. But instead of simply enjoying it, he stiffened. Stared. Swore under his breath. And stared some more. "What the -- ?"

He leaned over the railing to see better, and he wasn't smiling. That trim body was suddenly tense, and his hands gripped the railing so hard they turned white. I looked to see what had caught his attention.

What I saw was totally wrong. So wrong that it was terrifying as it slowly, inexorably filled the valley with horror.

I wanted to scream. I tried to scream. I couldn't. I couldn't even breathe.

I could only watch as a wind, roiling and many-colored and sparking like electricity came up the funnel formed by the valley. It was headed straight towards us. No, not just a wind. It was more than a wind, I could see that. It was composed of putrid clouds that billowed and turned in a tornado-like roll and was filled with fire sparking deep in it and growing exponentially as it rose along the valley.

It came slowly but deliberately. Inexorably. And it was heading straight for us.

There were vortices rotating inside the multi-colored cloud and those vortices began turning, slowly at first but then faster and still faster as the whole thing rose inexorably up the hill, growing more frightening and gaining speed as it came, even as the sparking grew until the entire cloud was a mass of fireworks.

The closer it got the better we could see the details.

The roiling mini vortices. The horrendous colors. The electrical discharges. The uprooted brush and entire trees that had been torn out of the ground and were circling in the approaching vortex. And it was headed towards us.

I could do nothing. I was frozen to the spot. Not so the military type. "Run!" he yelled as he moved even before I had time to react to the horror coming our way and think what to do.

But in the seconds since sighting the approaching cloud he'd somehow managed to turn, look over the area in that way he had that saw everything and in less time than I could possibly see half of it had assessed the entirety of the overlook and found the only safe place.

He pointed. He yelled again, knowing I wasn't in possession of my wits. "Between those rocks! It's our only chance!"

Without waiting for permission, he grabbed my hand and hauled me towards the rocks, running at top speed with his entire concentration on reaching those rocks. His thoughts didn't include me. I was incidental, a person who happened to be nearby when the world went crazy, and he dragged me along automatically.

I was familiar with the rocks we were headed towards. There were two of them, each twenty feet high at least with a narrow space between them that would provide the only safety in the overlook. I'd always thought of them as places for couples to make out. Now I saw them as the difference between life and death.

Somehow, I regained control of my body and got my feet beneath me and ran without being dragged. We both ran flat out. He jerked me ahead of him and I slid between the rocks and slammed against one of them as the military type slammed against me.

I hugged the bare rock as hard as possible, making myself as small as I could while he spread his arms wide on either side of me, his front to my back, protecting me against what was coming as he tried to push both his body and mine into that solid rock.

Then the wind hit. It was a living, breathing thing. It was both sound and fury and it howled with a sound that would have taken my breath away if I'd not already been holding it in sheer terror. It screamed like a banshee as those strangely colored clouds poured over the railing we'd been leaning against moments earlier full of currents that ebbed and twisted like monsters from hell. If we'd still been there, we'd not have survived.

The wind blew over and around the rocks we hid between and tried to penetrate between them but they were solid and no wind was a match for them. All that touched us was the cloud itself, diffusing and spreading between the rocks with strange colors and electrical charges. We were soon immersed in a multi-colored fog. Sparks flashed everywhere, pushed by that wind from hell. But the rocks kept the wind itself at bay.

We lived.

But we didn't survive unscathed.

Something happened as that vile air surrounded us. As it filled the space between the rocks, surrounding us and pressing against our bodies.

But it did more than that.

It passed through our clothes and into our bodies. Then it moved through one of us to the other and back again. From inside the man behind me to inside me and then in reverse, from inside of me back to inside of him.

Over and over again, in and out of us both, taking from me and giving to him and then taking from him and giving to me. I felt it in every atom of my being. The losing of myself and gaining him and that the same thing was happening to him. Whatever that multi-colored wind brought with it was inside of us. Both of us. At the same time.

But it wasn't just in us.

It changed us.

Somehow. Both of us.

I felt the change in my companion even as I felt it in myself.

I pressed harder against the rock and prayed. As I prayed, it moved through our bodies, each body separately and both bodies together, deeper and deeper until it reached the core of our beings. It was cold and hot at the same time. It touched every particle of our beings.

It wanted us. Both of us. I felt the wanting and knew the man against me, protecting me, also felt it. We were both afraid. Terrified. And there was nothing either of us could do except press harder against that rock and wait for it to end and hope we survived.

Then the wind moved on. The body that had been pressed so hard against me went slack as the wind died and the howling lessened and a few, faint beams of sunlight penetrated the space between the rocks. As those welcome beams touched us, the electrically charged fog lightened. Lessened. Then it gradually disappeared, and my body once again belonged to me and I no longer felt like I was joined with the stranger who'd experienced the wind with me. We were separate beings once more.

I followed his gaze and saw the cloud climbing past us, high and then higher still into the sky but it moved faster than it had climbed the valley and now that it had unlimited space in which to spread it grew thinner and weaker until, in less time than I could believe possible, it dissipated entirely, leaving the sky once again the soft blue of summer.

The gentle summer day was exactly as it had been before the wind came.

We separated and stood for a long time staring at one another until I asked, in a shaky voice, "What just happened?"

"I wish I knew." His voice, too, was unnatural. Of course, it was. "All I can say is that we just survived something out of a horror movie."

"Did you feel it? Was it inside us?"

"It was. I felt it too."

What was there to say to something like that? We stood in silence for a very long time as the sun came out stronger and we moved slowly, carefully, experimentally, out from between the rocks and into warm, welcome rays of sunshine. We were silent as we sought to come to grips with the fact that we'd both experienced the same absolutely impossible thing.

"But it's over." He spoke in a reassuring tone of voice that didn't fool me one bit. Did the military train people to pretend nothing was wrong when the world around you was coming apart? It must. "It's over and we're still here. Whatever it was, it's gone and we're okay and that's all that matters." Ignoring the fact that we were somehow changed.

We slowly moved back to the railing that we'd left in such a hurry. It was sturdy and had survived the wind but we had to pick our way through the mass of detritus the multi-colored horror had left.

Leaves, twigs, small and large branches, stones and larger rocks, and a lot of dirt had been sucked into the vortex and dropped as it lifted into the sky.

I pointed to the building at the bottom of the valley. "I think they do some kind of research down there."

"Do you think they made the wind?"

"No one knows what they do because they don't say and there are always guards at the entry so no one can find out anything. Hikers are turned away regularly."

I knew because the protesters had told me when they returned after the building was done and occupied. They came to make sure I knew the building represented evil incarnation and that if I'd helped prevent it from being built then that evil might not have come to our quiet part of the country.

My military type companion said nothing. He didn't respond to my accusatory tone of voice. But he did stare momentarily at the almost invisible building as if doing so would answer any questions he might have. Then he looked away.

I spoke again, not because I had anything to add but because I needed to talk to someone, anyone, and he was the only other person in the area. The only person who'd understand what I'd just experienced because he'd experienced it too and I needed to talk but couldn't bring myself to talk about the wind because it shouldn't have existed. So, I said the only thing I could think to say. "I'm Zoe Smith."

"Tate Brewster." We stared at each other for a long time because we didn't know what else to do. What to say. How to come to grips with what had happened. Then Tate Brewster cocked his head and considered me with an odd expression. I couldn't imagine what he was thinking as he looked me up and down, from head to toe and asked, "Would you do that again?"

I didn't know what he meant, and my puzzled expression showed it. "Would you introduce yourself again?" Seeing my confusion, he added, "I have a hard time remembering stuff. I'm terrible with names."

He lied. People like him always remember things they wish to remember. Of course, they do. An excellent, trained memory goes with the ability to see everything and think quickly in an emergency as he'd just done. Which meant there was a reason for his wanting me to repeat my name. I just didn't know what the reason was.

But I did as he requested. "My name is Zoe Smith." I gave Tate a questioning look. He correctly interpreted my look as asking why he wanted me to provide information he already knew.

He half nodded. "You are right. My request has nothing to do with actually introducing ourselves."

Then he did another odd thing. He introduced himself to me. Again. Just as he'd done less than a minute earlier. "I'm Tate Brewster." When I didn't react, he said, "Please, if you don't mind, let's introduce ourselves a third time. I'll go first. But this time when I say my name, watch my lips."

Tate Brewster repeated his name and as he spoke, I saw what he wanted me to see. What I'd not noticed until he called attention to it. What I couldn't avoid seeing now that I knew what it was. It was that obvious. And that scary.

I spoke to him very carefully so he'd know I'd seen what he wanted me to see. *"We aren't talking out loud. There is no sound. We are communicating with our minds and nothing else."*

He nodded. Without either of us uttering a single word, we'd introduced ourselves to each other. Just with our minds.

As the truth of what was happening dawned on me fear crept through my entire body. Sheer, unadulterated terror.

Then he spoke out loud intentionally, because we needed to hear each other. We needed sound. We needed normalcy. "How did we do that? Talk with our minds?"

I spoke out loud too, also intentionally, thinking before saying each word because I was deeply afraid and needed to know the world still worked in a normal way and that I could speak normally if I chose to do so. "What did that awful, horrible, weird wind do to us?"

Our next words were said together. By both of us. We spoke with our minds but we also used our voices. We spoke both out loud and mentally.

We stared at each other and made sure the other was staring back and paying attention as we asked the questions that were now the most important questions we'd ever asked. Ever. In our entire lives. "What has happened to us? What have we become?"